F   305
Bel Bell, W. Bruce
     A little dab of color

DATE DUE			

A Little Dab of Color
by W. Bruce Bell

A Little Dab of Color

by W. Bruce Bell

Lothrop, Lee & Shepard Books
New York

Library of Congress Cataloging in Publication Data
Bell, William Bruce.
A little dab of color.
SUMMARY: A young boy recalls life with his feisty grandmother who came to
stay after the birth of his baby brother. Loosely based upon the author's
boyhood in Indiana during the early 1900's.
[1. Grandmothers—Fiction. 2. Indiana—Fiction] I. Title.
PZ7.B4119Li   [Fic]   80-11986
ISBN 0-688-41956-9   ISBN 0-688-51956-3 (lib. bdg.)

FOR MARILYN AND A.J.

Contents

1   A LITTLE DAB OF COLOR   9

2   TRUTHFUL THADDEUS   30

3   GRAMMAW AND THE PEACH-TREE TEA   40

4   MY BROTHER'S KEEPER   63

5   SWIMMING-HOLE REUNION   82

6   A CAT NAMED JOSEPH   99

7   REED-ORGAN COWBOY   129

8   PUTTING ON STYLE   156

9   GRAMMAW CHANGES BEDS   173

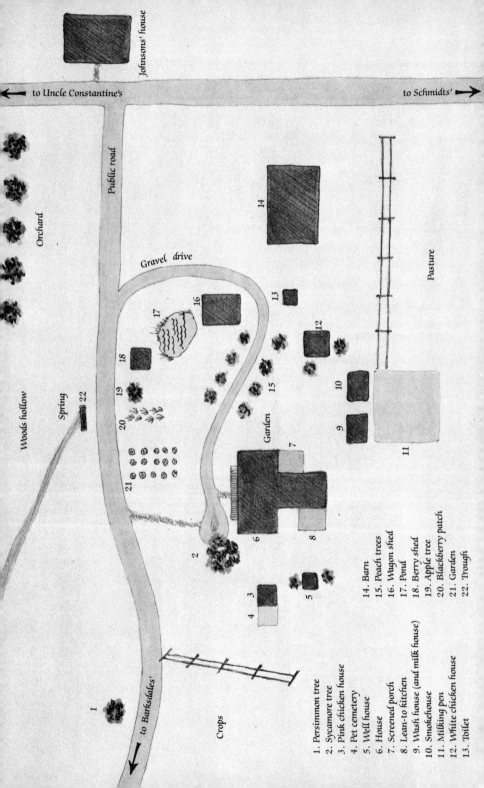

Johnsons' house

← to Uncle Constantine's   to Schmidts' →

Public road

Orchard

Gravel drive

14

Woods hollow

Spring   22

Pasture

17
16
18
19
20
21
13
12
15
10
9
11
7
Garden
6
8
2
3
4
5

11

1

Crops

to Barksdales'

1. Persimmon tree
2. Sycamore tree
3. Pink chicken house
4. Pet cemetery
5. Well house
6. House
7. Screened porch
8. Lean-to kitchen
9. Wash house (and milk house)
10. Smokehouse
11. Milking pen
12. White chicken house
13. Toilet
14. Barn
15. Peach trees
16. Wagon shed
17. Pond
18. Berry shed
19. Apple tree
20. Blackberry patch
21. Garden
22. Trough

1

A Little Dab of Color

AFTER ALL THESE YEARS I CAN REMEMBER AS WELL AS YES-
terday the sunny afternoon in March, 1914, that Grammaw Brown came to make her home with us on Pleasant
Ridge. It was the week after the Last Day of School and
an early spring had already touched up the beautiful hills
and valleys of the Indiana Knobs with a fresh coat of
green. Redbud brightened the woods hollow across the
road from our house, and dogwood bloom hung like new
lace curtains around the edge of every clearing.

For several days the wind had blown warm and dry
out of the southwest, unusual for this time of year. All
over the neighborhood you could see plumes of dust rising above the bare fields where men followed a team and
harrow working down the ground for summer oats.

My eight-year-old brother Hubert and I watched the
thermometer on the back screened porch. It climbed all
day. By the middle of the afternoon the mercury was
stretching up toward 70 and the line that marked "Summer Heat." We went upstairs and took off our copper-
toed shoes and black ribbed stockings and threw them
into a closet on top of the heavy long underwear that we
had secretly shed and thrown there the week before. The

official date for going barefooted was May 1, but on this afternoon there was no one to enforce the rule. Dad had gone to Grammaw's house at Horner's Chapel, twenty miles away, to bring her back to our place. Chod, the hired man, was at work in the fields. Mother was in bed with the brand-new, red-looking baby that Doctor Bodine was alleged to have brought in his black satchel sometime during the night. And today, at least, we could escape the supervision of our older sister, Devore, who had volunteered to act as Mother's nurse and was hovering around her with all the fussy attention of a hen with one chick.

Hubert and I went downstairs barefooted and minced across the porch to the front yard. The brick walk felt smooth and warm; the young grass felt coarse and springy to the touch of our tender, shoe-bound feet. A few days of running through plowed ground would toughen them up on the bottoms, and by midsummer they would be taking us over clods and gravel and turning briars and wheat stubble like the thickest of horsehide. The only drawback was that they would have to be scrubbed with soapsuds every night at bedtime. That was a cross every farm boy had to bear.

Being outdoors without shoes for the first time in spring made you feel as light and free as a puff of wind. Hubert said, "Last one up in the lookout's a rotten egg," and we went racing over the grass to the sycamore that stood in a corner of the front yard. Its lower branches were as thick as a man's body and so high that we had to jump to reach them. Above there, the flaky trunk shot straight up into the blue. An easy climb through the side branches—so well memorized that we could have done it blindfolded—soon brought us to our lookout in the top, where four limbs grew horizontally out of the trunk toward the four points of the compass.

It must have been five stories above the ground, for we were up at least twice as high as the lightning rods on the house roof. We each straddled a limb and leaned back against the cool, slender trunk and looked at the familiar landscape. The whole country glistened, as though it might have been created only this morning and spread out in the warmth of the sun. Over our barn roof toward the east were the Johnsons' green-tinted apple orchard and red brick house buried in puff-ball shade trees, one of them marked by a small dark speck near the top where our pal Thaddeus had sawed out a few limbs and built a tree house. In the far end of our south pasture a herd of what looked to be toy cattle grazed across a green crepe-paper slope. Beyond them stood the Schmidt house like a white and chocolate-brown dollhouse neatly placed among building-block cribs and barns. To the west a field of young rye shimmered in the wind, pale green on bottle-green, like a piece of changeable silk. On a knoll beyond the far edge of the rye field stood the Barksdale house, where the yard was overrun with sawbriars, coonhounds, and little kids in wet diapers. Barksdales were the neighborhood poor folks. But this early in the year, before the weeds grew, their old mustard-colored house and unpainted buildings looked tidy. There were no houses to the north of us. Beyond our spring hollow, it was all Knobs and covered with trees. The surface of the

Knob woods rolled away to the horizon like a wide green
ocean, with cloud shadows coasting over the crest of the
waves and down into the trough like phantom ships.

Up there in the tip-top of the tree you rode back and
forth on the sway of the long trunk that tapered up from
the ground. You seemed to belong to the open sky, the
same as the crows that flapped past and the lone buzzard
floating above the woods. That lookout was the scene of
most of our make-believe games. Sometimes we were Jim
Hawkins and other characters from *Treasure Island*.
With bandanas tied over our foreheads and butcher
knives stuck under the suspenders of our overalls, we sat
and charted the spring hollow for places to bury pieces
of eight and chests of old bones. Or we were Robinson
Crusoe and Friday, shading our eyes with one hand and
anxiously scanning the Knob Woods for a full-rigged
schooner to come sailing down the wind to our rescue.
And after I read *Knights of the Round Table* we'd had
a bitter dispute and some vigorous hair-pulling over
whose privilege it was to be Sir Galahad and have the
pure heart and strength of ten.

The lookout was not only an entertaining place, but
useful as well. When a thunderstorm gathered in the
southwest we could observe whether it was coming our
way or going around. If it came straight on and we saw
lightning flash over the tin roof of the schoolhouse two
miles away, we could scoot down and advise Mother, and
she could drive the brood hens and baby chicks into their
coops before the rain fell.

Even farm work could be interesting when viewed

from so remote a place with no danger of becoming involved. In fields all about us in haying time we watched the loading wagons grow fat as they crawled forward and consumed the winrows. We saw wheat shocks spring up and dot the yellow stubble floor in the wake of the grain binder. We saw the wigwams of fodder shocks arise where the long parallel stripes of corn rows had been. On the morning when the smooth brown surface of a harrowed field was washed over with light green we knew the winter wheat was coming up.

We also had a fine overall view of traffic on Pleasant Ridge. Ordinarily, it was the buggies, surreys, and farm wagons of our neighbors, pulled along the red clay lanes by horses or mules, that were as familiar to us as their owners. Sometimes a caravan of strange black wagons appeared (gypsies!), and then we were careful to stay in the tree until they had gone, for we thought it was safer there. If we saw the glass sides and rounded top of the hearse at the head of a long procession of rigs, we climbed down and went out and stood respectfully on the edge of the road while it passed.

Every vehicle that came from the west had to pass the Pleasant Ridge church, which stood around the next bend of the road and across the way from the Barksdale house. Willow trees grew on each side of the road there and made an arch overhead. Any rig that approached could first be seen in the little dark spot amidst the willow trees, which was shaped like the opening of a tunnel.

This was the place we watched impatiently every weekday morning for the appearance of what looked like a big

square cereal box on wheels—the mail wagon. Dan, the
fat roan gelding that pulled it, was so fat and pokey that
Mother would have plenty of time to finish a letter or
make out a money order before he arrived. And if
"Uncle" Milburn, the mailman, had a postcard bearing
a message that he deemed of importance, he would drive
up to the house and deliver it rather than risk the mail-
box.

The most exciting thing of all, and one that always
happened when you least expected it, was to see an automobile scoot out of the tunnel like a runaway surrey that
had become unhitched from the horses. Then we slid
down from the tree in a shower of sycamore bark and ran
full tilt to the road so that we could stand dangerously
close when it chugged past.

This March afternoon we had a special reason for
watching the willow trees. Dad would come back that
way from Horner's Chapel and, unless something had
happened, Grammaw would be with him. Grammaw had
finally accepted Mother's invitation to come and live
with us. Her other daughters wanted her, too, especially
our rich Aunt Clara, who lived in faraway Evansville,
but Grammaw had chosen to come to the farm.

At this time we were not too well acquainted with
Grammaw. We remembered from her visits that she was
little and old and lively and set in her ways. Everybody
knew that when it came to grandchildren she was partial
to girls. All of her own children had been daughters.
Now that she was moving in for good, it was bound to
make a difference in the lives of Hubert and me.

The sun was sliding down behind the weatherbeaten belfry when at last Old Nellie's white face and mane appeared. The buggy came around the bend, dipped down out of sight in the hollow at Barksdales' place, and in a little while it cleared the hilltop where the big persimmon tree stood along the edge of the rye field. We recognized the small figure beside Dad on the seat.

"She's with him, all right!" Hubert cried. "It's Grammaw."

We waited until the buggy had passed the spring hollow and gone on up to the barn-lot gate. Then we climbed down out of the tree and ran to meet it on the driveway.

Grammaw sat as stiff and straight as a beanpole under her little skillet-shaped black hat and long mourning veil that fell in many folds from the back of it. Although the day was warm, she was dressed all in black: black silk pleated shirtwaist with a choker collar, black gloves, and a heavy black crepe skirt. Grammaw, we knew, didn't dress according to the weather. Winter and summer she wore mourning for Grandpa Brown, a man who meant no more to us kids than a whiskery tintype on the parlor whatnot and a big granite tombstone in the Horner's Chapel graveyard. Grammaw differed from the widows around us on Pleasant Ridge. They were beginning to wear gray and sometimes lavender and would gradually taper off into half-mourning, as it was called. Grammaw wouldn't cater to these changing styles. She wore solid black all of her life, just like what she was wearing on this March day. Grandpa Brown had then been dead twenty years.

Grammaw was looking this way and that as she rode up the driveway, cocking her head from side to side like a pert mother blackbird examining a new spot for a nest. She had always liked our farm, but she showed a keener interest in everything now as her glance darted to the sprawling green-shuttered house, the picket fence, the garden, and the cluster of whitewashed buildings in back. She had just sold her old home place after fifty years of housekeeping, and so there must have been sadness in her face, too, that Hubert and I were too young to notice.

Anyhow, Grammaw didn't give us time. She hopped out of the buggy almost before Old Nellie could stop. While Dad was setting out her baggage she rooted through her handbag and found a striped paper sack. She extracted two sticks of horehound (like brown glass braided and pressed flat), gave us boys each one, and said, "Merciful Father! What dirty faces! A-body could tell your mother was sick and not able to look after you. Barefooted, in March! You'll catch your death of cold on this damp ground. My, how much you boys favor each other. Like two peas out of the same pod."

It was true that Hubert and I looked alike. I was two years the older, but Hubert had grown faster, and we were so much the same size that strangers often mistook us for twins. Several of our kinfolks called me Hubert and him Bruce, thinking that a boy in overalls was just a boy in overalls, so what was the difference? Nothing could have made either one of us madder. Grammaw knew us apart, all right, but she had her own names for us. Grammaw always spoke a split second before choosing for sure the one she was going to address; as a result she called us Bru-Hubert and Hu-Bruce until we were grown.

"Bru-Hubert," she said now, pointing to the pasteboard cartons that Dad was lining up on the grass, "bring some of them boxes in the house. Both of you go and wash your hands before you eat that candy, and your faces. Hu-Bruce, you carry this basket and that poke with the potted geranium in it. Careful you don't break the leaves. And you boys get your shoes on the first thing."

She picked up her canvas telescope valise and disappeared through the front door. She had given us so many confusing orders that Hubert and I thought it best to let them wait until they could be sorted out and placed in order. Chomping on our horehound, we followed Grammaw empty-handed into the house.

She went to the bedroom off the dining room, where Mother lay with her arm around the new baby. Devore sat at the bedside brushing Mother's hair, which fanned out over the pillow like a black silken shawl.

"How are you, Lulie?" Grammaw asked, kissing Mother and pulling down a corner of the blanket to peer at the baby. "Another boy, just like I told you it'd be. Hmph! Pretty little trick, though. Favors William around the eyes. I bet they'll be brown, too. But he's got your dimples."

Grammaw exchanged a stick of horehound for the hairbrush in Devore's hand and sat down by the bed.

"Wash your hands before you eat that. Raise this window a wee bit more. Did you get along all right?" The question was for Mother.

"Fine. I'm strong as a mule. I was sorry you couldn't be here this time. William had to run for one of the neighbor women. This little fellow wouldn't wait. He almost beat Doctor Bodine."

"He rushed the season, too, didn't he?" Grammaw said, referring both to the baby and to the hot March weather.

Hubert and I stood in the door listening to the talk. It was mostly about what had taken place the night before, but of course in terms acceptable to the ears of boys who still presumably believed that babies came in the doctor's black satchel. We didn't reveal that we knew better. We sniggered when Grammaw finally asked, "Devore, how'd you make out with the cookin'?"

Mother smiled, too, and said, "Devore, show Grammaw the biscuits you baked for breakfast."

Devore beamed and brought in a plateful of little white discs as thin and hard as the china that held them. Hubert and I showed Grammaw how we could roll them on the floor like saucers.

"Let 'em tease all they're a-mind to," Grammaw said. She thumped one of the biscuits. "It 'pears to me you left out the soda. You're only—what is it, twelve? I'll show you how to bake bread that'll make their mouths water." But for a long time Grammaw saved a dozen of those first plaster-of-paris biscuits as a souvenir of Devore's first culinary attempt.

"That reminds me," Grammaw said, jumping to her feet. "I better change my duds and take a-holt if we are going to have any supper."

She grabbed her valise and skimmed upstairs to the spare bedroom. The first thing I noticed when she came back without her hat and veil was her hair. It seemed to have grown tighter, somehow. Grammaw didn't consider hair "A Woman's Crowning Glory," as the magazine advertisements for Sutherland Sisters Tonic called it. Hers, although a beautiful silken white, was just something to shampoo twice a week and keep up out of her face the rest of the time. Her way of dressing it was to stretch it up hard and tight from all around, fasten it to her scalp with side combs, and wring it into a severe little milkweed pod on top.

She had changed to a starched calico dress. It was black, of course, and relieved by the tiniest of white figures, because Grammaw observed mourning in her everyday clothes also. What looked odd was not the black dress but the apron she was tying over it—a big blossomy affair the color of sheet lightning, with wide sashes in back and a hem that brushed the floor. This was the first in a long series of flowered, polka-dotted, and striped aprons that identified Grammaw from then on, even though you were a mile away. You never saw her around the place without one. Grammaw loved to be surrounded by brightness, so much in fact that she was soon poking red crepe paper in the fonts of all the coal-oil lamps to give our rooms an extra touch of color. Seeing this, you realized how much she loved Grandpa, dressing herself in dead

black to the end of her days in his memory. An apron
didn't count. Grammaw allowed herself this exception
on the grounds that an apron was not so much a garment
as the trademark of a housekeeper.

Her shoes were like those she had worn when she first
arrived, although older and shabbier—her third best pair.
This was another of her habits that time revealed. Grammaw never bought any kind but those soft, comfortable,
high-laced black shoes, and she always had exactly four
pairs. The first for Sunday best, the second for slip-on
when company came, the third for every day, and the
fourth—with broken tongues and crooked heels—was kept
in the woodshed and worn when she walked to the barn
in muddy weather or ventured to the fields to pick a
kettle of wild greens. She replaced her Sunday shoes from
time to time, and all four pairs were shifted down the
line one notch. I used to wonder what happened to the
oldest, or bottom, pair when it was thus crowded out of
service. Then one day I saw her burying them under the
grape arbor. "Rotten leather makes fine fertilizer for
grapes," she told me. Later on, I found this to be true.

Grammaw finished tying her apron sash and trotted to
the kitchen. Her tiny presence filled it with sound and
activity: the rattle of dishes, the swish of soapsuds, the
clank of pots and pans. When we came back from doing
the chores at the barn we could hear the sizzle of ham in
a skillet. The smell of bubbling coffee and hot biscuits
greeted us at the door. The big square table in the dining room was spread with a fresh blue-checkered cloth,

and Grammaw had arranged a handful of yellow Easter flowers in an empty sugar bowl in the center.

"Bru-Hubert," she said. "Pull up the chairs. Supper's on."

Dad sat on one side next to the vacant place that Mother would occupy as soon as she was able to be up. Hubert and I were opposite Grammaw and Devore, and the whole lower side was given to Chod, who needed plenty of room to spread his arms. Grammaw brought the granite coffee pot and set it at her elbow on an upside-down pie tin. She pulled the hanging lamp down until its circle took us all in. We bowed our heads. She began, "We give Thee thanks, O Lord . . ."

And Grammaw was one of the family.

Hubert and I were satisfied that Grammaw had joined us for keeps when Dad went lumbering away in the farm wagon to Horner's Chapel the next morning and drove it home that night full of her furniture wrapped in old quilts.

The big vacant room at the head of the stairs seemed to have been waiting for Grammaw. Devore and her dolls and quilt pieces occupied the room just back of it, and Chod had the little den at the rear. Hubert and I slept in the west front room across the hall from Grammaw.

For the floor, she had brought the light matting of natural straw from her former living room. The wallpaper she had put on, a cream color with bold yellow tulips, was really kitchen paper since she'd dismissed the pale sprigs and rosebuds of the bedroom paper samples as having "no body to 'em." The furniture unwrapped from the quilts was all pieces she'd prized too highly to part with when she'd sold her house. The four-poster walnut bed, an heirloom from her childhood home, stood in a corner, puffed so high with straw tick and feather bed that Hubert and I wondered how Grammaw would get into it: whether she would use a stepladder or do as we boys would have done: climb to the top of one of the carved posts and retire belly-whopper-style. She put the Seth Thomas clock in its glass case, a wedding present, on a stand table near the door. The platform rocker, where she had rocked her five baby daughters to sleep, went near a front window so she could sit and rest behind the lace curtains and look out in the yard without being seen in her dressing gown.

Besides all the furniture there were chair tidies and pillow covers (pieced from scraps of silk the size of your thumbnail) and pincushions and calendars (long out of date, but hung for some sentimental reason) and little odds and ends and bits of color that made the big room seem as cozy as a bird nest. During the long time she lived in it, the room looked precisely the same as it did the day she first placed her house slippers under the rocking chair and her white and blue flowered chamber pot (which she called a "vessel") under the walnut bed. A stranger would have called it a comfortable place, though perhaps a bit confusing. But Grammaw could walk in there in pitch dark and lay her hand on the fan or knitting basket she wanted. After you knew Grammaw, you understood why. She chose the exact and only spot for an object she wished to keep. Then, like her superstitions, her love, and her wardrobe, it was fixed for life.

Grammaw had been with us about a week when Mother got up from her bed. She was well and strong and ready to tackle the spring housecleaning and all of the garden-making that baby Wilson's arrival had delayed. Mother had told Dad she would ask Grammaw to help her in little ways about the house. What she'd actually said was, "I'll let Ma potter around if she wants to, and make her think she is helping me with the housework." That was the proper way to treat a woman of Grammaw's age, she thought: let her feel useful and then she would never worry about being in other people's way. But Grammaw was already several jumps ahead of her, as Mother soon discovered.

One day Mother sat down to nurse baby Wilson and she happened to think that she had forgotten to sweep the front porch. Going later with a broom, she found that the porch had not only been swept but scoured. Even the brick walk to the front gate was wet and steamy from a recent scrubbing. "Of course I did it," Grammaw said. "I 'loud you'd be busy makin' your lettuce bed."

A week later, Mother finished planting peas in the garden and hurried to the kitchen to start getting dinner. The potatoes were peeled, and a fire roared away in the cookstove. Grammaw was hustling around. She ruffled up like a setting hen preparing to peck somebody who had invaded her nest. She said, "I'll get dinner. Why don't you stay out in the garden where you've got work of your own to do?"

Grammaw didn't intend to potter around—she intended to take over. And to her way of thinking, if anybody worried about being in the way in the kitchen, let it be Mother.

So it came about that first spring, and by no means gradually, that Grammaw became the housekeeper and left Mother free to work outdoors. A farmer's wife on Pleasant Ridge never had to search for ways to keep busy, especially on a big 240-acre farm like ours, with cows to milk, butter to churn, hundreds of baby chicks to hatch, and the garden to tend.

Mother was an outdoor woman. She was small like Grammaw and darted about with the same skimming motion (which reminded you of a busy quail), but she was sunburned and rosy-cheeked and had such a look of strength about her that you were likely to think of her as tall and robust. She was, to tell the truth, happy to let Grammaw take care of the house.

Grammaw had kept house for fifty years in a five-room cottage. Turned loose in our roomy farmhouse, she was like a little bitty whirlwind in a forty-acre field. If you happened to be where you couldn't see the flash of her apron, you could stand still and locate her by the noise: the whack of a carpet beater in the backyard, the bustle of a feather bed on its way to the front veranda for an airing, or the squeal of casters in an upstairs room as she trundled the furniture about and hunted dust.

After the wind from the housecleaning had died down you could retrace Grammaw's path. Bright sofa pillows and patchwork tidies had popped up behind her like crocuses. And it wasn't long until color showed up outside, too, because Grammaw was a great hand for flowers. She borrowed Chod from the corn planting and set him to spading up a wide strip of sod all around the yard inside the picket fence. Hubert and I helped to break the clods and pulverize the soil in exchange for the fishing worms. One of the numerous pasteboard cartons in Grammaw's luggage produced canna bulbs. Another held her favorite dark red dahlias. In the bushel of old aprons brought along to cut into carpet rags she had carefully packed several glass jars of flower seeds. Out of them came four o'clocks and flowering sage and coxcomb and zinnias and about every other garden flower you could name. That year and every year afterward, from early summer until frost blackened the last cosmos, Grammaw's flowers made bright ribbons of color inside the picket fence.

Several of the outdoor jobs had been delayed that spring on account of baby Wilson, and the one that Mother wanted most urgently to get done was the whitewashing. Mother and Hubert and I had begun it the first of March. We'd whitewashed the chicken house that stood by the two sweet cherry trees back of the garden, and now it showed up as bright as a new dollar against the green foliage. But the baby was born then, and we'd postponed the rest of it. Hubert and I were not the kind of boys to work without strong moral support and close personal supervision (in other words, every chore we performed was forced labor), and whitewashing was a job that even Mother dreaded. We still had to do the other chicken house, a huge woodshed, the smokehouse, the little shed over the well, and the building next to the milking pen, which housed the cream separator and the laundry equipment. These all had to be gone over each year, and so did the kitchen, which was a board and batten lean-to on the opposite side of the dining-room wing from the screened porch. The kitchen had never been painted; so it was always whitewashed to match the color of the rest of the house.

Mother liked to have all this done early in the spring; she said a fresh clean coat of white on the buildings made the place look like somebody lived there. The trouble was, it wouldn't stay fresh and clean. The sun faded it, the rain streaked it, and next spring it was all to do over. Mother asked Grammaw if she knew of a way to make whitewash stay on longer.

"Yes," Grammaw said. "You put a right smart of salt with the lime and then sift in some wood ashes. Makes it stick like paint."

"Wood ashes? Won't it be gray then, instead of white?"

"Add some Venetian red. That covers up the gray. Of course, your whitewash will have a kind of a pink tinge. But that ought to look good with your white house and dark green shutters."

Mother ordered the Venetian red the next time our huckster neighbor, John Schmidt, made his weekly twenty-mile trip to New Albany (or, as everyone said, to Town, in order to distinguish it from the village of Borden that lay in the valley five miles to the north). He brought a fifty-pound bag of powder that was as fine as soot and a deep maroon in color. Mother picked a cloudy day to apply the whitewash, so that it would dry slowly and not peel. She rounded up Hubert and me and three brushes and prepared to mix the stuff in a barrel in the backyard.

"Ma," she called. "How much of these extra ingredients do you put in?"

"Just guess it off," Grammaw called back from the kitchen, "the way I'm makin' my sponge cake." Grammaw seeemed to cook entirely and successfully by guess.

Mother, on the other hand, was inclined to overguess. She stirred in a great quantity of salt and wood ashes; then she had to use the whole bag of Venetian red to balance out the gray. Pink tinge or not, she wanted this batch to stick on for at least two seasons. Hubert went to the west chicken house, I took the smokehouse, and Mother climbed on a stepladder and began the kitchen. The sun stayed behind the clouds all day. It had already disappeared below the willow trees at the churchyard when we finished the last long swipes on the woodshed and cleaned our brushes. The buildings were still damp and spotty, and Mother remarked about their peculiar rusty gray color. Of course, you can't look at wet whitewash and forecast the results; often a thin dirty-looking coat on old wood will dry out to a dazzling white. Mother said she hoped it wouldn't rain during the night and spoil our work. It didn't.

At sunrise the next morning we were just getting up when the telephone sounded a fast long-and-two-shorts, our ring. Mother answered. From upstairs we heard her say, "Quite well, thank you. How are all your folks, Lettie? . . . *What? Oh, no!* I can't *help* being excited. Thank you, Lettie."

Bang! went the receiver. Mother came running across the screened porch to the back hall door and called upstairs, *"Everybody-get-down-here-at-once! Lettie-says-our-whole-place-is-on-fire!"*

"Merciful Father!" Grammaw screamed. "Wait till I get dressed."

She darted out of her room shaking her skirts in place and went and dragged Devore from her bed. Chod's big eyes and wild hair appeared at the back bedroom door. Hubert and I slid down the banisters. (This time it was justified.) We all reached the kitchen at the same time. Dad grabbed Wilson from his crib, and in a few seconds we were out in the yard, prepared to run for our lives.

We found no blazing timbers, no fire at all, not even a wisp of smoke. But it took only a moment to see where our neighbor Lettie Johnson had made her mistake, and why she had sped to her phone without a second glance at our place. She had merely gotten a glimpse of the reflections when the rising sun lit up the new whitewash. The kitchen and the five outbuildings had dried out in the night to a glittering American Beauty pink.

We didn't know it that morning, but our pink whitewash was to stick on so well that for years people used it as a landmark. If a stranger came to Borden and asked for directions to a farm on Pleasant Ridge, he was told, "Drive up the valley road till you come to a steep knob. Climb the knob and then bear left. Go about three miles and you'll see a place that you'll think is on fire. That's Bells'. . . ."

The salt and wood ashes and Venetian red had done the trick. Grammaw walked over between the kitchen and the woodshed. It was shady there, and above the dew-wet grass the air itself appeared rose-colored.

"Well, I'll swan," she said. "There's more of a pink tinge to it than I 'loud there'd be." She looked up critically at the house and then at the cluster of American Beauty buildings. "But it does go good with the white paint and dark green shutters. I always say nothing keeps a-body in good spirits like a little dab of color around a place."

2

Truthful Thaddeus

GRAMMAW'S INTRODUCTION TO THE MORE TRYING ASPECTS
of life on Pleasant Ridge was not complete until she met
Truthful Thaddeus. This happened shortly after she arrived, and I wish I could say that first acquaintance
ripened into close friendship. Thaddeus and Hubert and
I played together almost every day, and it was generally
at our place because we had more acreage to explore and
a bigger barn with higher lofts for jumping into the hay.

Thaddeus was the only child of Big Sam Johnson and
his wife, Lettie. Looking at the parents, you would have
wondered where they had obtained Thaddeus. Lettie
was a mild little iron-gray woman who would never be
noticed in a crowd. Big Sam was lanky and weatherbeaten, and without the stoop to his shoulders would
have measured a good six feet three. Both of them were
truthful, hard-working people.

Thaddeus was short and chunky and conspicuous, and
freckled like a turkey egg, and his hair was the color of
a burning brush pile. He was a year younger than I and
of course a year older than Hubert, and if he had wished,
he could have whipped both of us put together. Thaddeus could run the fastest, jump the highest, throw the

farthest, and stay under water the longest of any boy on Pleasant Ridge. At the risk of character assassination, I'll have to state that he was as lazy as Hubert and I were.

The neighbors called him Truthful Thaddeus, with mild sarcasm, as they would have referred to a perpetual swindler as Honest John, and for comparable reasons. Thaddeus's skill at prevarication even overshadowed all of his athletic accomplishments, due to the fact that he practiced it more often. When accused by the neighbors of taking part in mischief of some sort, his alibis were marvels of invention, but accepted by his mother as gospel truth. Lettie told the informants, politely but firmly, that they were mistaken. Thaddeus had denied it, and therefore he was innocent. "He wouldn't lie about it," she insisted. "That wouldn't be Thaddeus."

Nevertheless, Thaddeus was our best pal. Hubert and I envied the way he could use his imagination to save his hide, just as we envied him his skill with his fists. He was also a fine ringleader, although Hubert and I could have managed with a poor one. We ring-led easily.

Trouble seemed to brew faster than usual when the three of us were together. The rocks we threw at sparrows were more likely to go through the kitchen window, or hit Grammaw's chamber pot where it hung in the sun on the cow-lot fence. We would forget that we were forbidden to wade in the horse trough at the spring, and Dad would find it all riled up at watering time and the horses would refuse to drink. We'd play shinny too close to Grammaw's canna beds and leave them looking as though somebody had camped there overnight. And one time after Thaddeus had come down and described a camp meeting revival, we accidentally baptized three of Mother's best Dominecker roosters to death in the pond back of the berry shed.

As a catalytic agent, the closest runner-up to Thaddeus was Cousin Eddie, the son of a distant relative of Mother's. There were eight other children in Eddie's family, and not much income. To relieve his parents, Mother and Dad often let him spend a few summer weeks at our house doing odd jobs. He was thin and weasel-faced, about fifteen or sixteen years old, and such a storehouse of secret and wicked adult wisdom that even Thaddeus looked up to him. He sang dirty songs and added liberally to our stockpile of profanity. And by taking us in the cow stable at the proper moment he had disproved Mother's black satchel explanation, at least as far as it concerned newborn animals.

Grammaw had quickly acquired a kind of immunity to Cousin Eddie's ways, but after three months of almost daily exposure to Truthful Thaddeus and his talent for fiction, she was becoming more and more irritated with him. One June afternoon Dad sent Cousin Eddie to the barn to oil a set of harness. Hubert and Thaddeus and I had been playing tag in the barn loft, and after coming down for a drink of water at the well, we stood around watching him. He had the harness strung up on pegs over the workbench and was rubbing it with a rag dipped in machine oil. Every once in a while he would turn his head aside and proudly spit a brown stream on the barn floor. Chewing tobacco was his latest adult pursuit.

Thaddeus asked him what fun he got out of chewing. Eddie said he didn't really like the taste of tobacco. The only reason he chewed the stuff was to grow hair on his chest.

"Will that do it?" we all asked in one breath.

Sptiu! Eddie squirted a jet of tobacco juice into the chaff and wiped his chin. He said, "Didn't you ever notice Chod with his shirt off? How do you reckon he got all that hair on his chest? Eating bread crusts?"

It made sense. Chod was both the hairiest man and the heaviest chewer on Pleasant Ridge. Often he ran out of tobacco between trips to Borden. When this happened, he'd send Hubert and me hopping across the pasture to the country store kept by our other neighbors, the Schmidts. We'd stand in the storeroom and watch Mrs. Schmidt place the long black slab of Star tobacco under the horizontal knife and swing the lever down like a pump handle to slice it off into pocket-size plugs. Our only interest had been in the trademark, a five-pointed star pressed into the center of each plug. These and the tiny horseshoes and other labels were collected by all the boys and prized as ornaments for everyday straw hats. We'd carry the tobacco to Chod without the slightest temptation to try it. And until Eddie mentioned it, we had never thought to connect Chod's chewing habits with the fact that what we could see of his chest above an unbuttoned shirt looked like a forkful of hay.

"Will it start sprouting right away?" Thaddeus asked.

"There's one thing about it," Eddie answered, studying a leather tug of the harness, "tobacco won't ever grow a hair till you're man enough to chew it." *Sptiu!*

I said, "What if the folks find out? Remember how Grammaw caught us smoking corn silks."

"Yeah," Hubert said. "But you know how she happened to find us. We sent up so much smoke she thought the privy was on fire. Nobody can tell we've been chewing tobacco."

Thaddeus said, "If they notice anything I'll say we've all been chewing dried grape leaves."

Beyond a doubt, Thaddeus could lie enough for three people. Still, we hesitated. It seemed like a serious step to take.

"Hell," Eddie scoffed. "I don't think you kids ought to chew. You're all too little. You wouldn't look good with that much hair on your chests."

That cinched it. We told Eddie to hand over the tobacco.

Eddie said, "Now remember, I'm not making you chew. You're sure you want it?"

We were sure. Eddie pulled out the plug he had stolen from Chod's overalls on the back porch. He said the older men told him the bigger the chew, the thicker the hair. We all bit deep.

"Hey, wait a minute," Thaddeus mumbled, rolling his chew in place with his tongue. "Will mine be red like the hair on my head, or black like Chod's?"

Eddie passed the tobacco to him again. "Well, Chod uses better'n a plug a day, and his hair's black as coal. You can figure it out for yourself."

Thaddeus decided to try for coal black. He bit off another chunk.

We started a game of hide-and-go-seek, feeling like regular old tobacco chewers already, and wondering how soon we could look for the new upholstery to appear on our chests. Hubert's face and mine were lopsided, with a big quid tucked in one jaw; Thaddeus's wad in each cheek gave him the look of a freckle-faced chipmunk in hickory-nut season. We ran and got hot and drank freely at the well in back of the barn. Of course we took care to swallow every time we felt like spitting. Cousin Eddie said if we did this we could expect the results sooner.

My first result was to notice that something peculiar had happened to Thaddeus. There were two of him, sliding apart and then sliding back together and blending. I looked around to ask Hubert if he had seen it, and found Hubert doing the same thing. Suddenly both pairs of them leaned against the two corncribs and tried to throw up. They made a lot of loud gagging noises, but neither seemed to be getting any material results.

Strange as this was, I couldn't make myself take an interest in it. All I could think of was the load of cherry cobbler I had eaten for dinner, and I began to wish it was faraway. For the first time, I noticed how stuffy the air had become inside the barn. Going outdoors was harder than I thought. The sweat was running down in my eyes, and the door looked small and distant. About this time, the barn started going around, not fast, but with a lazy floating motion, and once in a while a corner gently dipped up and down like the Ocean Wave ride at the County Fair. I lay down on a pile of corn fodder and thought wearily that I would get up and hurry through the door the next time it came around to the front.

I heard Mother yelling for Grammaw, and after a short time I heard Grammaw's voice: "Merciful Father. All three of 'em. Oh, Lulie, what shall we do? They've been poisoned on something."

I saw their faces, far off and centered in little ripples, like faces reflected in running water. Faintly, I heard Mother say, "No, they aren't poisoned. I think I know the trouble. See that dark brown stain around their mouths? Eddie! *Oh, Eddie!* I'd like to know where he went in such a hurry. I thought he was oiling harness. Let's try and take the boys to the house."

They held Hubert between them and went dragging out of the barn. Sometime later, they came for me. Grammaw put her arm around me on one side, Mother on the other. I could feel them pulling and half carrying me up the gravel driveway. I knew I wasn't much help, for my knees seemed to have been fitted with swivel joints, and they kept swiveling the wrong way.

Hubert was stretched out on Mother's bed like a small forgotten corpse. They heaved him over and stretched me out beside him. For all I cared, they could have thrown me down the well. The only thing I wanted was to get rid of my cherry cobbler. Mother questioned us about what we had been doing.

"Chewing dried grape leaves," we said feebly.

"Leaves, that I believe," Mother said. "But it was some flavor besides grape. Haven't you been chewing tobacco?"

Hubert and I confessed at once. We both wanted to die with a clean conscience, even if we couldn't purge our stomachs first.

Mother said, "You'll have to suffer the consequences. This will be your punishment and, I hope, your cure."

She bathed our faces and necks, and the cool water gave us some relief. Mother and Grammaw had started to the barn for Thaddeus when Grammaw stepped to the telephone and cranked a short-and-a-long for Johnsons'.

"I think Lettie ought to see her boy alongside of ours," she said.

She told Lettie over the phone that Thaddeus was quite sick at his stomach. Nothing serious, oh no, but they were going to put him to bed for a while, and then maybe Lettie would like to come down and walk home with him.

Lettie lost no time. She came at a run through their apple orchard and across the wheat field. She arrived as Mother and Grammaw were bringing Thaddeus into the backyard.

Lettie screamed at the sight of him. His red hair was sticking out from his head every which way, like a thatched roof hit by a cyclone, and the pea-green face under it just didn't seem to belong. He had tobacco juice all over his freckles, for he was too weak to hurdle his chin

when he tried to spit. Overambition about the color of
the hair on his chest had been his undoing. He was moan-
ing and gagging something fierce.

"Oh, I'm sick." *Bloooo-oooop. Buuuu-uuuurp.*

"Yes, honey, I can see that."

"Oh, I'm gonna die." *Wuuuu-uuuurp.*

"Thaddeus, honey, what in the world happened?"
Lettie asked, helping Mother and Grammaw labor him
up the back steps. "What's that brown stain on your
face?"

"I chewed up a few dried grape leaves."

"But was it the grape leaves that made you so awful
sick at your stomach, honey?"

I raised my sick head and listened closely. I knew that
Thaddeus's talent wouldn't desert him, even at death's
door. Between groans, he explained to Lettie that he
had been playing in the hayloft with his mouth open
and accidentally swallowed a tumblebug. Lettie didn't
bother, as Mother would have done, to ask what a tumblebug would be doing away up in a hayloft. A tumblebug's wings are too small to carry its big hard-shelled
body more than a few inches off the ground. About the
only way you ever see one travel is crawling backward
along a cowpath, pushing a hard round ball of dirt and
manure toward home with its scaly hind legs. But Thaddeus claimed he'd swallowed a tumblebug, and so it was.
He didn't lie. That wouldn't be Thaddeus.

"Oh, how sickening," Lettie exclaimed, retching at
the horrible thought, as they rassled Thaddeus through

the bedroom door. He flopped down beside me like a bag of turnips, loosely packed.

Lettie said, "Grammaw Brown, you're so good at fixing up all kinds of remedies. Can't you give the poor child something to make him throw up?"

"No, Lettie, I can not," Grammaw retorted and, sick as I was, I could detect an undertone of satisfaction in her voice. "This time he'll have to tough it out like the others. If a tumblebug wouldn't puke a boy—Merciful Father!—I can't mix up anything that would."

3

Grammaw and the Peach-Tree Tea

MOTHER HAD QUICKLY BEEN CONVINCED THAT SHE MIGHT as well give Grammaw free rein in taking care of the house; so she turned over to her all the responsibility and reserved for herself only one important job. Even so, Grammaw flew off her handle every once in a while and threatened to replace Mother at that one, too. I mean the job of switching us boys.

Punishing the kids was just as much a part of the housework on Pleasant Ridge as making the beds and washing the dishes except, of course, it had to be done a great deal more often. Only the meanest of boys were ever whipped by their fathers, and usually this was in a family where the father set a pretty ornery example himself. All the boys in our neighborhood were kept in the paths of righteousness by their mothers. Different women favored different methods of persuasion.

Mother preferred peach-tree tea for Hubert and me. She didn't box our ears and run the risk of injuring us, or take down our pants and run the risk of blistering her hand. She liked a peach-tree switch because it was flexible and easy to handle; it held up under use without snapping in two; it had no hard bud knots to leave pockmarks on the skin. Her choice may also have been affected by her fine source of supply. It was one the neighbor women envied.

Two rows of seedling peaches grew along our driveway between the house and the barn. A dozen or more trees bordered the curve of the garden fence, and about the same number followed the edge of the truck patch on the opposite side. They were frowsy-looking trees, and an orchard man would have noticed that they were top-heavy as a result of pruning the lower branches too much. The blossoms made a pink, bee-busy lane out of the driveway in the springtime, and the fruit set on early, but it never lived up to its promise. The peaches were mostly peeling, with a bit of tough, yellowish meat welded to a great big seed. For eating out of hand, Hubert and I used them only to mark time until the Early Elbertas ripened. Besides being worthless for bearing fruit, the trees drew a lot of strength from the soil, so that vegetables planted near them along the edge of the garden or truck patch failed to make. Dad spoke every year of chopping them down for firewood. Hubert and I volunteered our help with a speed we didn't ordinarily show when firewood was mentioned. But Mother wouldn't have allowed the trees to be cut down for anything.

"Oh, no," she said. "Leave them awhile. Let's wait and see how the boys are going to behave this summer." So the trees stayed by the driveway and covered themselves every spring with a fresh crop of long willowy shoots. And since our behavior followed the same pattern season after season, fall of the year always found

their lower branches stripped off again as naked as a
picked hen.

Hubert and I took our peach-tree tea the same way we
took any other kind of medicine. Hubert put it off until
the last minute and tried to make believe that he could
avoid taking it. I accepted it at once and tried to make
believe that I might thus be given a smaller dose.

The way Hubert postponed it was to light out and
run away from Mother. She always had to chase him
down like a game rooster before she could switch him.
The chase usually took place in the yard. I can just see
them now: Hubert burning the wind around the house,
with his bare feet hardly touching the grass; Mother
coming lickety-split behind him, with her dress tail crack-
ing in the breeze, while she waved a long switch and
warned Hubert that he had better stop and take his
medicine before she got good and mad. Mother sort of
ran wide; that is, she bore out well to the middle of the
yard to avoid colliding with somebody at a corner. Hubert
took more of a chance. He ran next to the house or, as
you might say, on the inside rail, and he had the advantage of a much shorter distance. In spite of that,
Mother's endurance was more than a match for Hubert's
early speed, and he always got what was coming to him
in the end.

I wasn't the kind of a person to exert myself unneces-
sarily. I was the one who tried to reduce the dose. I stood
meekly and waited for Mother. When she raised her
switch I bent over, *awa-a-a-a-ay* over, and shrank—in
pretty much the same hunkered-up shape a cow assumes

when she swings about and presents her tail end to a rainstorm. Then at the first light tap across my back I screamed bloody murder. "Ouch! Oh! Oh! Stop! Don't kill me! Mother, ple-e-e-ease don't kill me!" I made sure that my words could be clearly understood across all the hills and hollows of Pleasant Ridge. I hoped that Mother would quit for fear the neighbors would rush in and accuse her of trying to beat one of her children to death. I might as well have saved my voice. There were a lot of boys being brought up on Pleasant Ridge, and so this same kind of a protest could be heard coming from almost any backyard in the neighborhood when the wind was right.

Neither of our tricks ever cut any figure with Mother. She decided on the amount of punishment we deserved and that was what we got. And we had been taking her kind of tea for so long that it seemed like an old and reliable remedy—like sulphur and molasses, for example—awful bitter when you took it, but perhaps of some benefit in the long run. We hated to think of changing our brand.

But now here was Grammaw, with her high-handed and energetic way of doing everything. She hadn't been at our place two weeks when she began to threaten that she was going to grab a switch and lay it on us, and since she was in charge of the housekeeping she had every right to do so. Hubert and I decided that it was best not to provoke Grammaw to the point of giving us our peach-tree tea, for everything hinted that it would be an overdose.

To begin with, Grammaw had always carried a chip on her shoulder for Hubert and me. If she'd had her say-so we wouldn't have been boys at all, sassing our elders and talking rough and littering up the house. By rights, Grammaw figured, we ought to have been girls, in starched calico, fiddling with doll buggies and learning to piece quilts. That was what she'd prophesied before we were born.

During her visits to our house each time that Mother was expecting, Grammaw would tell her whether the baby was going to be a boy or a girl. Many women of her generation claimed this same power, basing their prediction in some way on the shape of the pregnant woman's waistline. Before Devore was born, Grammaw had assured Mother and Dad that their baby would be a girl. She hadn't stopped there either. I don't know what she used as evidence, unless the signs were right in the zodiac, or maybe she guessed; but she'd also said she felt certain that the baby would have a lot of dark brown hair and brown eyes like Dad's. She would be pretty as a picture, Grammaw had added.

Devore had filled the bill exactly. At the age of one year she took first prize in a baby contest. And now at twelve, she was exceedingly pretty, quiet, well-mannered, and already an expert with needle and thread; in short, possessed of all the qualities that were sure to make her a grandmother's favorite.

Two years after Devore was born, and again two years later, Grammaw had repeated her prophecy. Those times she came all the way from Horner's Chapel to help Doctor Bodine bring us into the world. She'd arrived each time prepared to welcome another granddaughter—a pretty girl with dark eyes and long brown hair that she could twist around her finger in little spit curls. What she'd gotten instead was first me and then Hubert, both of us born bald, blue-eyed, and *male*! There were all of our yard-long infant dresses and petticoats, embroidered and knotted with dainty ribbons, and the piles of jackets and bootees and stuff that Grammaw had knit with so much confidence—everything in the wrong color. You couldn't have blamed Grammaw for being aggravated when Doctor Bodine had said, "A boy."

Of course Wilson was a boy, when Grammaw would really have preferred the fourth baby to be a girl. But she had prophesied a boy this time, and Wilson got off to a good start with Grammaw by conforming to the rules. Besides, he had the dark curly hair and big brown eyes that her forecast always favored, and so Grammaw never harbored any grudge against Wilson.

Hubert and I had contradicted all of the old time-honored signs by not being brown-haired, brown-eyed girls, and Grammaw couldn't see that we were doing a thing to make up for this dirty trick. Our eyes were still the same robin's-egg blue as hers and Mother's; and Grammaw was highly partial to brown. We had Grammaw's quick temper, too, and Dad's lean, wiry frame and strong hands, without a trace of his inclination to apply them to something useful. We also had several features, such as straight hair-colored hair, snub noses, and big feet, that Grammaw's search of both family

trees failed to account for. One of us would have been
bad enough, but there were two of us, and Grammaw
couldn't help feeling that we had ganged up on her.

It was several years too late to change our sex, but
Grammaw seemed eager to work us over in other ways.
"You just try sassin' me again," she would snap (or invite us to repeat whatever other offense we had committed). "I'll get me a switch and I'll raise welts on you."
The tone of her voice made us think of bright red welts
the size of a lead pencil. When she was more provoked
than usual she went so far as to say, "You do that one
more time and I'll cut the blood out of you." As soon as
she was familiar with the way we reacted to one of Mother's switchings, her threats were worded to suit our in-
dividual habits. "Bru-Hubert, if I have to whip you I'll
bet I make you wish you *could* run." And: "Hu-Bruce,
you just hide another lizard in my sewing basket and
I'll take a switch and give you something to screech
about."

One of our disadvantages—one from which Thaddeus
never suffered—was that Mother had a highly efficient
Crime Detection Bureau, composed of a big sister and
a hired man. Often when we played in the barn or the
spring hollow she sent Devore along to monitor our
frequent lapses into profanity and other departures from
the straight and narrow. With all of her other virtues,
Devore had keen eyes and ears and a dependable talent
for reporting. Chod was equally alert and informative.

Circumstantial evidence of our misbehavior also had
as much weight with Mother as eyewitness testimony.

Like the time we were accused of exploring in Chod's room—and later in Grammaw's.

We called it exploring, but the family insisted that it was rummaging. And the same kind of thoroughgoing curiosity that got Drake and Magellan in the history books only got us another ample dosage of peach-tree tea.

We had made an exhaustive study of Chod's cubby-hole under the dining-room roof. There wasn't much to explore: some work clothes, chewing tobacco, a bare-bellied Kewpie doll from the County Fair, and his Sunday suit with nothing in the pockets but matches, a knife that wouldn't cut hot butter, and the same old mushy letters signed "Your Darling Ethel." What really attracted us to Chod's room was his alarm clock. With the alarm wound tight, you could twist the setting hand until it clicked, and then you could turn the bell on and off to play streetcar, taking turns at being motorman and conductor. Unfortunately, we had to skin out in a hurry one day at the sound of footsteps in the lower hall, and we neglected to reset the clock. Later, when the alarm aroused Chod, he reached out and shut it off, groped about in the dark for his clothes, and went to the barn and fed and watered and harnessed the horses at one o'clock in the morning. He grouched about it until Mother found a key for his door.

By contrast, Grammaw's room was a treasure trove. We liked to unfold her pretty painted paper fans and fan ourselves. We took the postcards out of their transparent envelopes and fingered the familiar bluebirds, puffy red roses, and heavy raised letters of powdered tin-

sel that said "Happy Birthday" or "Merry Christmas."
We pawed through her button box and knitting basket,
climbed a bedpost, and dove into her feather bed. Then,
under a stack of neatly folded nightgowns in the bottom
dresser drawer, we chanced one afternoon to come upon
her bottle of Cashmere Bouquet toilet water. We poured
out dripping handfuls and rubbed it on our arms and
legs, sprinkled it on our shirts and overalls. Our noses
gradually got used to the sting of it, but when we sat
down at the supper table the whole family declared that
our fragrance was almost unbearable. Grammaw said,
with feeling, "You let me catch you rummaging in my
dresser drawers again, and I'll switch you like you've
never been switched."

And so Hubert and I worried a great deal that first
summer of Grammaw's arrival. We never knew when
Grammaw might be pushed too far and suddenly carry
out her threat. She wouldn't stop to think it over first
in Mother's calm, levelheaded way. Grammaw was exactly as calm and levelheaded as a firecracker when she
got mad and, like the firecracker, the bang was out of all
proportion to the tiny size of the package.

The showdown came one day that fall when Mother
and Dad were away from home. Hubert and I got in
trouble with one of the neighbors, which was always a
dangerous thing for a boy to do if he prized his hide.
The folks wouldn't stand for any mischief that might
result in hard feelings with a neighbor. Grammaw had
to meet the emergency and she didn't have a moment
to think it over. We boys never forgot it.

The neighbor was Constantine Temple, an old widower who lived with his four grown children and raised strawberries on a small rocky farm to the east of us. Everybody called him Uncle, which was the common way of showing respect for a man's age or his standing in the community. Uncle Constantine had both. He was dried-up and ancient, with a cream-colored beard that could easily have been tucked under his belt; and with the doubtful exception of God, he had the most influence of any man in the Campbellite congregation of the Pleasant Ridge Church. Hubert and I sometimes tried to imagine him wearing a flowing Old Testament robe instead of the cast-off Sunday clothes of his three sons that he always wore for every day. Then, we said, hand him a stone tablet bearing numerals from one to ten, and he would be a dead ringer for Moses as our *Stories of the Bible* pictured his coming down from the mountain.

Uncle Constantine's children were Matthew (age 48), Mark (46), Luke (44), and Miss Johanna (who admitted that she was around 30). Matthew, Mark, and Luke were all serious and religious like their father, and it wouldn't have surprised us to learn that they had simply stepped out of the Scriptures and started hoeing strawberries, instead of actually being born and growing up. If they had ever been young boys, Uncle Constantine had forgotten about it. He didn't like children. He reserved all of his love for Jesus and the grown-ups, and the only interest he took in small boys was to watch them like a hawk watching a chicken and then report to their parents any mischief that was likely to get them a switching. So naturally, the relations between Uncle Constantine and the neighborhood boys were more than a little strained.

Since he was so crack sure of going to Heaven whether the rest of us did or not, we thought we'd give him all the Hell we could before he left. For most of us boys, this was fairly easy. Several times a week Uncle Constantine made the five-mile trip down in the valley to Borden. He drove a faded apple-green jolt wagon and a team of faded red mules, as old as the hills and as slow as the seven-year itch, named Luther and Wesley, a swipe at Uncle Constantine's favorite religious enemies. The most popular way of teasing him was to hide in the sassafras bushes by the roadside and throw clods or rotten fruit at him as he drove past. Another favorite form of ammunition was road apples dropped in the dust by passing horses. A dry road apple shattered in a thousand pieces when it struck its target; so Uncle Constantine was kept pretty busy on the road to Borden and back, combing fragments out of his beard. Of course he went and told the boy's parents that he had been hit with a "piece of—er—ahem—horse dung," and the boy was the one who suffered. Teasing an old man, especially a religious old man and a good neighbor, there was no excuse for it, the grown-ups claimed, and the boy always got a hard thrashing, which Uncle Constantine loved to watch.

Hubert and I had always escaped. We used more refined ways of pestering him. Not because they were more refined, but because they were safer.

After Uncle Constantine drove out of the lane that led

from his farm past Johnsons' and turned onto the main
road, there was a long straight stretch past our barn lot.
Hubert and I stayed inside our fence and barely glanced
up as he came jogging along, quoting Scripture to himself in a loud voice and gently gouging Luther and
Wesley in the rump with the soft butt end of a blacksnake whip to keep them from falling asleep. Out of the
corner of our mouths, we boys called, "Whoa," and the
mules surprised Uncle Constantine by stopping dead
still in the road. They were a little less hard of hearing
than he was. Maybe it was because they were a few years
younger than his seventy-odd, or maybe it was because
they had slightly longer ears, but one reason or the other
enabled them to pick up sounds that Uncle Constantine
couldn't quite catch. When we softly called whoa they
would come to a standstill, and Uncle Constantine didn't
know why. He said, "Giddup," and gouged them in the
rump. They mosied ahead. We called whoa. They
stopped. Uncle Constantine used a big portion of his
driving time getting past our place by these short hitches,
wondering what on earth possessed old Luther and Wesley that morning, while Hubert and I busied ourselves
at some innocent game on the other side of our barn-lot
fence.

This finally led us to another stunt that was more of
a challenge to our skill. After the road passed the barn
lot, it dipped down between the truck patch and the
upper end of the spring hollow. Hubert and I would
run ahead of the wagon, and as soon as we reached a
place where the elderberries hid us from the house we

started cutting across the road in zigzags. When the mules caught up with us, we were ready to dart catty-cornered in front of them, missing their long whiskery noses by about the width of a hair. Luther and Wesley tossed their heads high and sat back in the britchin straps, and even though they were going slowly the sudden backward lurch threw Uncle Constantine to the front, and he had to grab the seat to keep from pitching out of the wagon.

He stood up and cracked his blacksnake whip at us in righteous indignation. Not the soft butt end he poked the mules with, but the business end that he kept oiled and ready for bad boys. We had to jump out of its way in a hurry, for his skinny arm was long and much more powerful than you would think. If we misjudged his reach or failed to jump fast enough, the braided rawhide tip stung like a coal of fire between the shoulder blades.

Uncle Constantine knew that if he went and told Mother we tantalized him she would put a stop to it. For that reason, he kept quiet. Sometime, maybe the next time, a boy was going to be caught off his guard. Then what a privilege it would be to wrap the whip clean around him and give him something to remember. One blistering lash of a blacksnake whip was equal to a dozen of Mother's peach-tree switches, and it could easily have raised one of the red welts that Grammaw was always talking about. Uncle Constantine held on to his whip and bided his time.

So on that memorable day in September when Mother and Dad went to the fair and left Grammaw in charge of us kids, Uncle Constantine decided his time had come. It was Saturday, and Mother had saved for us the job of picking the last of the dry beans. We went ahead and picked them without too much fussing, for she had promised to bring us Cracker Jack and candy as a reward.

Right after dinner Grammaw asked us why we didn't go and see if we could find enough ripe persimmons to make a pudding for supper. She said she would sack up the beans and when we came back they would be ready for us to hull, as we usually did, by clubbing the sack about the yard in a game of shinny. Hubert and I snatched a gallon bucket apiece and sped toward the woods. Gathering persimmons was an activity that could possibly be placed under the heading of Work and therefore to be avoided, but we didn't stop to split hairs. The pudding would be worth the effort. When you sat down at the table and spooned into a slab of Grammaw's baked persimmon pudding—rich, cocoa brown, and thick, topped with whipped cream and a sift of nutmeg—you could just about hear the angels sing.

There had been a heavy killing frost the night before, the kind that was needed to remove the last trace of puckery flavor from the ripened persimmons. Later that day, the sun had warmed up enough for Hubert and me to peel off our shoes and stockings and roll up our overalls for one final day of making believe that it was still summer.

We went to the woods and filled our gallon buckets with the sweet, mellow fruit; our stomachs were something like half full when we came back across the rye stubble to the big old persimmon tree that stood in the edge of the field above the cherry orchard and spring hollow, not far from the dividing line between us and Barksdales'. The tree grew out of a steep bank where years of weathering and slow traffic over the road had sliced a deep gulley between the fields. We climbed the dead roots that lay against the bank like ladder rungs, skinned up the trunk, and went out on a lower branch that spanned the road as straight and level as a length of building timber.

We had been sitting astraddle of the limb and spitting persimmon seeds down into the road for perhaps an hour when, looking over toward the east, we saw two pairs of flapping mule ears and a familiar white beard coasting along the top of the sassafras bushes that marked the lane from Temples'. The team and jolt wagon and Uncle Constantine appeared at the corner and turned down the road in our direction. He was wearing Matthew Temple's old blue serge Norfolk jacket, too short at the wrists; Mark's old brown pet-top trousers, too short at both ends; a pair of Luke's old white buckskin shoes, slashed across the top to make room for his bunions; and an old everyday straw hat that looked like it might have been a relic handed down in the family.

Usually, Uncle Constantine recited Bible verses as he jogged to Borden. But this afternoon he was in a gayer mood. He was singing. He had to sing at the top of his quavery voice, for he was pretty deaf, and the old wagon made a terrible rattle. From our place high in the persimmon tree, Hubert and I got the benefit of every word. Uncle Constantine finished "Aunt Dinah's Quilting Party" as he turned the corner. His next song, "Silver Threads among the Gold," was interrupted several times as he drove past our barn lot. The mules were so in the habit of being stopped along there that every few steps they halted and cocked their ears sideways, just to make sure that somebody hadn't called whoa from the other side of the fence and they had failed to hear it above the concert.

"DARLING, I AM GROWING OH-HOLD," Uncle Constantine told the world. "Giddup there, Luther! . . . SILVER THREADS AY-MONG THE GO-HOLD . . . Wesley! Giddup! . . . SHINE UPON MY BROW TEW-DAY, TEW-DAY. . . . Luther! Wesley! Git a move on you! . . . LIFE IS FADING FAST AY-WAY. . . . What in tarnation ails you old mules, anyhow? GIDDUP!"

They finally passed the barn lot, and the wagon came rattle-ty-bump down toward the spring. By this time Uncle Constantine had changed his tune again. He had also reversed ends on his blacksnake whip, and he sat holding it ready for a couple of boys to dart suddenly across the road.

"MY BONNIE LIES OVER THE OCEAN," his high voice echoed up and down the spring hollow. "Blasted little imps of Satan; bet they're hidin' in them bushes." He peered into the elderberries. "MY BONNIE LIES OVER THE SEA. . . . Too big for their britches, that's what's a-matter. . . . MY BONNIE LIES OVER THE OCEAN. . . .

Ought to be took down a notch or two. . . . OH, BRING BACK MY BONNIE TO ME. BRI-I-I-ING BACK . . . BRI-I-I-ING BACK . . .''

Uncle Constantine laid his whip on the seat, for he had come to the end of the elderberries, and there was no danger of us flashing out of some shady spot and cutting across the road in front of the mules. He made a few remarks about the beautiful day. Then he started a little argument with himself, in a shout of course, because he wanted to hear both sides. It must have been part of a conversation that had taken place between him and the blacksmith about shoeing one of the mules. He kept yelling, "I SAID THE RIGHT FRONT HOOF, MR. HADDOX. I SAID THE RIGHT FRONT HOOF."

There was something about overhearing a man talk to himself that made the act seem a bit indecent, almost like spying on a naked person. This may have been one of the reasons why Hubert and I decided to stay sitting on the persimmon limb and listen. It would be more fun than stopping the mules or dodging the blacksnake whip. All we had to do was pull our legs up out of sight and he would never see us among the leaves.

Uncle Constantine settled his argument with the blacksmith. He rode in silence for a few minutes, and then he raised his voice and started quoting Scripture. The wagon thumped and clattered up the hill toward the persimmon tree. Above its noise we heard all of Psalm 23, followed by the Beatitudes.

Hubert and I tucked our feet under us and waited. We giggled at the thought of Uncle Constantine, red in the face from shouting and singing, driving right smack dab under us, screaming Bible verses at the top of his lungs and never dreaming that two hated boys were so close they could have reached down and pulled his hat off his head.

The long, rusty backs of the mules swayed over the wheel tracks. Their whiskered noses were almost in the shade of the tree when Uncle Constantine began Psalm 121: " 'I WILL LIFT UP MY EYES UNTO THE HILLS, FROM WHENCE COMETH MY' "—his patriarchal gaze swept up from the horizon and came to rest on the limb where Hubert and I were crouched a few inches above his face—" 'HELP.'

"Ah-ha," he said, leaving off the psalm and reaching for his blacksnake whip. He brought it up and over his head in a great lashing circle. *Swoooooosh. Kuh-rack!* The sinewy leather coiled around the limb between our bare legs.

Hubert and I let out shrieks and jumped, without any thought but to get beyond the reach of the whip. Hubert landed on one side of the road and I on the other, just clear of the mules' hind feet.

Luther and Wesley were shuffling through the dust with their eyes half closed, listening to the music and the Sunday school lesson from the wagon seat. About the last thing in the world they expected was two screaming animals to come dropping out of the tree into the road at their heels. With a surge that pulled Uncle Constantine right out from under his hat, they leaped a clean ten feet and ran away.

Uncle Constantine rocked backward, his bony grass-hopper knees bobbing up higher than his head. He dropped the whip and grabbed the wagon seat. The old wagon made a long apple-green streak over the brow of the hill behind the flying mules, with the wheels seeming not to touch the ground, while Uncle Constantine sawed on the lines for dear life and hollered, not a Bible verse, but, *"Whoa, gosh blast it. Whoa! Whoa!"* The last thing we saw as they disappeared below the sassafras on the far side was his cream-colored beard standing back over his shoulder like a banner in the wind.

Hubert and I got up out of the road and limped to the house. Our feet and ankles were stove up from the hard fall, but we both felt that the entertainment we had had was easily worth the pain. We found Grammaw in the backyard stuffing the beans into a two-bushel feed sack.

"Merciful Father!" she said. "Look at your filthy over-alls. Did you boys waller in the big-road? These beans are good and dry; they ought to hull easy. What are you two sniggerin' about? Must be something funny about them persimmons."

Hubert said to me under his breath, "Whoa, gosh blast it, whoa," and we held our sides and rolled in the grass to keep from bursting.

In a little while we heard the wagon coming back over the hill at its customary slow jolt. That would be Uncle Constantine on the hunt of his straw hat and his blacksnake whip. Luther and Wesley had shot their wad, as we knew they would. Their ancient muscles couldn't take them farther than the Barksdale place at that high speed; by the time Uncle Constantine had come to his senses and put on the brake they were both ready to stop.

Hubert and I lay on the ground and listened as the wagon left the persimmon tree. We waited for it to turn around and rattle off toward Borden again. Instead of that, it came down the hill. We looked at each other, guessing why. A slight difference in the scrunch of the wheels notified us when it left the dust of the main road and struck the gravel inside our barn-lot gate. It continued up the driveway.

Grammaw tied the bean sack, set it against the kitchen wall, and went around front to see what Uncle Constantine wanted. Hubert and I followed, strongly suspecting the reason for this call.

Uncle Constantine sat like an ancient king on his green throne of a wagon seat. As we expected, he was wroth. He was so wroth, in fact, that he couldn't even see straight, and he had crammed his straw hat on his head hind side before. He scowled under the jaunty off-the-face back brim and said, "How'd do, Mrs. Brown. Mrs. Bell at home?"

"No, she's not, Mr. Temple. Anything I can do for you?"

"I got bad news. Them boys hid in the persimmon tree up the road just for spite and caused my team to run off."

Grammaw said, "Tell me how it happened."

The facts were all in Uncle Constantine's favor. Hubert and I had to admit that we were hiding in the tree,

and not on business, because we had already filled our
persimmon buckets. We were both lame, so we must
have jumped. The mules ran away; that made us guilty.
Uncle Constantine was a religious old man; Hubert and
I were only a couple of boys and always in a scrape.
Causing a runaway was no light matter.

Grammaw said, "What do you want me to do about
it, Mr. Temple?"

"Spare the rod and spoil the child. I want you to whip
'em."

"Can't you wait and let their mother take care of it?"

"I want 'em tended to right now, while I'm here to
see that justice is done." He coughed. "Unless you think
you can't handle 'em by yourself."

Grammaw said, "I won't need your help, thank you."

She went to a peach tree, reached up, and yanked off
a switch. It was a whopper. The way her eyes snapped,
this was going to be the whaling she had always threatened
to give us.

"Bru-Hubert," she said, peeling off the leaves, "come
and take your medicine."

Grammaw seemed to have forgotten that Hubert was
the one who always took his medicine after a hard run.
He hightailed it around the house, and Grammaw trotted
after him, shaking her switch. She had hardly disappeared
when Hubert crossed the front yard on his second lap.
That was where Grammaw outsmarted him. She stopped
behind the house. Hubert was used to making a race out
of it, for when Mother got her dander up she was a swift
runner. Before he thought what he was doing he ran on

back and overtook Grammaw. She nabbed him.

Uncle Constantine's eyes lit up, and well they might. You never heard such a thrashing as the one Hubert was getting. The lash of the whip was all that could be heard, for anybody could have switched Hubert to death and he wouldn't have uttered a sound. After a while he came to the front yard.

"Grammaw says for you to come around there."

I humped over and got my voice ready for distance. At the corner I put both arms up over my face and went backing up to Grammaw like a land terrapin in reverse.

"So you teased the old man, did you?" she shouted. "Ain't you ashamed? This is what you get."

Looking under the crook of my arm, I saw her raise her whip, and I shut my eyes and braced myself. I heard an awful whack, but I couldn't feel it. All at once I remembered seeing a little cloud of dust hovering over the bean sack as I backed around the corner. It didn't take me long to catch on. I let out a string of bellows like a bull under the dehorning knife. The louder I yelled, the harder Grammaw punished the beans. Together we made enough noise to please Uncle Constantine. Grammaw led me around to the front yard. Her face was as pink as the kitchen whitewash.

"Well, Mr. Temple," she said, "the way I look at it, justice has been done. Good day to you, sir."

Uncle Constantine said, " 'Foolishness is bound up in the heart of a child; but the rod of correction shall drive it far from him.' Proverbs 22:15."

He combed his fingers through his beard, gouged the

mules, and rode down the driveway, looking from right
to left.

"THEM'S MIGHTY FINE PEACH TREES," he told himself
confidentially above the noise of the wagon. "Luther!
Wesley! Giddup!"

Grammaw fixed hot Epsom salts water and put us boys
to soaking our sore feet. She threw a towel down on the
floor between us.

"Now I want you both to use that. You just try leavin'
your big wet footprints on my clean linoleum. I'll take
that switch and I'll cut you to the red."

She glared at us and went outside. We heard the tinkle
of hulled beans pouring out of the feed sack into a tub.
Hubert and I felt a great sense of relief, and it wasn't
altogether in our feet.

4

My Brother's Keeper

AS FAR AS CORPORAL PUNISHMENT FROM GRAMMAW WAS concerned, Hubert and I knew that we were safely over the hump, and we could disregard her future threats. Then she began using moral suasion as a means of improving our conduct, and that was a different matter.

She had been trying various experiments along that line for over a year, and without any notable success, until one sultry hot Sunday in June when Hubert and I seemed to outdo ourselves at mischief, partly because on the Sabbath we had no farm work except a few light chores to occupy our minds and muscles or, as Grammaw put it, to keep us out of devilment.

Mother had spent so much of the day running with a peach-tree switch to end our fistfights that she no longer investigated the old alibi, "He hit me first." She laid it on both of us impartially.

Then Grammaw intervened and solemnly warned us of a worse punishment to come. "You know what happens to boys who disobey their elders and fight like two banty roosters on the Lord's Day? Well, the Old Scratch keeps an eye on evil-doers, and the first chance he gets, he carries 'em off. You mark my words, the Old Scratch'll claim you if you don't mend your ways."

"Yes'm," we sassed her. "Who told you so much?"

Toward evening, Grammaw called us to the kitchen and said she wanted us to fetch some water from the spring, which was located down in the hollow across the road below the truck patch. "Now see if you can do one thing today without creatin' a ruckus," she said. "Try to act like little gentlemen. But hurry with the water. I want to put the coffee on for supper."

Hubert ran down the path, with the intention of beating me to the spout where we caught the water. I climbed the fence and sped catty-cornered through the truck patch. We met near the lower gate and raced shoulder to shoulder for the spring. I jabbed my elbow in Hubert's ribs and sidetracked him into a blackberry bush. The briars delayed his bare feet long enough for me to cross the road and run down the spring hill a few steps ahead of him. Being there first, I leaned over the trough to place my bucket under the spout. Hubert came up from behind and gave me a hunch that sprawled me flat in the horse trough.

I wrung some water out of my clothes and stood aside while Hubert caught his bucket full. I thought I would act like a "little gentleman," as Grammaw had asked us to do. Besides, Hubert had a rock in one hand, and a rock is hard to dispute. Hubert set his bucket of water on the ground and climbed out on an oak limb to skin the cat. My bucket was filled before he knew it, and I loped up the hill and left him hanging wrongside-out on the limb. He yelled that I had to wait for him.

We had a sort of taken-for-granted rule that one of us would never go away and leave the other on the scene of a piece of work, even if it was only where we caught a little drinking water. But when Hubert said "wait" he meant that I must stand still in my tracks until he passed around and walked in front, where he could stop suddenly and force me to bump into him. I thought of "waiting" as merely slowing my pace so that he could almost but not quite overtake me before I reached the kitchen.

I was waiting in my usual way, at a moderate walk about middle ways of the truck patch, when Hubert ran up behind me and pitched a clod at my bucket. Hubert was known for his good aim. The water swirled up muddy and brown as the clod sank. I stood still until he caught up with me, pretending that I didn't know what he had done. The water was dirty and unfit to drink and so, to save Grammaw the trouble of pouring it in the canna bed, I poured it on Hubert. He gave me a hard shove. I caught a big toe in the cuff of my overalls and tumbled into the dust between two sweet-corn rows. I happened to have a tight grip in Hubert's hair at the time, and he went down on top of me.

Mother was sitting on the front porch. She came running.

With Mother and a peach-tree switch on our heels we went to the house. She gave us clean clothes and made us go to the spring one at a time. Then she sent us to the barn to shell corn for the chickens, with a warning to behave or suffer the consequences.

A fight erupted when I pointed out to Hubert that he was picking out the long, easy-shelling ears that were for the horses, instead of the nubbins Dad wanted shelled for the chickens, and he responded by breaking a large, easy-shelling ear over my head. Mother hurried to the barn and promptly gave us everything she had promised. I looked at the faint pink stripes on my legs afterward and felt that Hubert had ruined my whole day.

After supper we were lying on our backs in the front yard, watching the chimney swallows circle around and drop to the roost in the parlor chimney. I said, "I think I'll climb up to the lookout and watch the moon come up."

Hubert said, "That's just what I was going to do. I get the east limb to sit on."

We broke and ran for the sycamore tree. I hoisted myself over the bottom limb and started to shinny up the trunk. Hubert grabbed my ankle and swung his weight on it. I gave him a kick with my free foot, not a hard one, such as I would have applied to the regular kicking area, but a firm backward thrust of my bare foot in his face to loosen him. Hubert turned a somersault across the limb and fell straight to the ground. He stretched out and lay still.

All the doors of the house burst open at once. Out came Mother and Dad and Grammaw and Chod, followed by Devore carrying little Wilson. Dad knelt down and examined Hubert. He found no broken bones. He tried to coax Hubert to say something. Hubert was dumb (and in this case only do I mean "unable to speak"). He didn't utter a word. Mother sent Devore scurrying to the kitchen for a washcloth and some water to bathe his face. Devore was beside herself with excitement; she grabbed a dishrag and a pan of buttermilk. It felt cold, and before Mother realized what she was doing she began to swab Hubert's face. Hubert hated buttermilk. He promptly sat up to spit. I saw Dad wink at Mother. She said, "Carry him to the screened porch and lay him on the lounge. He'll be all right."

Hubert hung down from Dad's arms as limp as the wet dishrag while he was being carried to the porch. Dad had no more than arranged him on the lounge when he raised up and demanded a cup of tea and several crackers. (Coffee was the everyday beverage at our house; tea was a luxury, kept under lock and key and served only to visitors and members of the family who were recovering from an illness.)

Grammaw put the tea on to brew, and then she spoke her mind. She stated it directly opposite from the way she meant it, as she often did to show that she was washing her hands of a problem she couldn't solve.

"I want you boys to go ahead and fight like heathens. Fight till you get your belly full of it. See if I care. I won't have to listen to it. I'm goin' over to visit Barbara Schmidt till things quiet down around here. She clapped her little black hat and veil on her head and prepared to leave. "And if you boys don't take to doin' better I don't know as I'll even stay here one more summer. I'll move to Evansville and live with your Aunt Clara, where a-body can have some peace." She stalked off across the pasture toward the Schmidt house.

Mother and Dad had been preparing to go to church when the accident happened. A revival was in progress and Mother was obliged to go because her clear soprano voice was the mainstay of the choir. She told Dad she could manage Old Nellie and the buggy if he wanted to stay and look after Hubert.

Dad said, "Hubert is convalescing just fine. All he needs is more tea. I'll go with you."

"Yes, but the boys will fight. Ma went to Barbara Schmidt's, you know."

"We can avoid that by taking Bruce with us."

Mother said, "Bruce, go and wash with soapsuds—certainly, your feet, too—and put on your Sunday clothes. You're going to church."

Dad said, "I think you might profit by listening to a good sermon."

The revival was being conducted by a Brother Thomas, an elderly, shouting evangelist of a visiting denomination. He was said to have backslid and been reconverted a countless number of times.

Brother Thomas announced his topic as "Sin and Punishment." After the Scripture reading he stood and tugged on his goatee awhile, and said abruptly, "You're a sinner!" It startled me so that I jumped.

"Yes, brethren, you're all miserable sinners in the sight of God. . . . Every day you go astray, and you

think maybe God won't notice it this one time. . . .
But he does, my friends. . . . He knows every little
secret sin in our hearts and He never forgets. . . .
PRAISE GOD! AY-MEN!"

I began to fidget with uneasiness, wondering how
Brother Thomas had found out so much about me. I
knew I was guilty of a few sins, little bitty ones, but I'd
always hoped that God was too busy with other matters
to bother about them. I expected that on the Judgment
Day he would dispose of them the same way farmers
handled odds and ends when they advertised a public
sale. After the livestock and farm implements had been
described, these miscellaneous things were always lumped
together in a line of small print at the foot of the sale
bill: "Other items too numerous to mention."

Brother Thomas made it clear that God didn't trust
to memory or just lump things together. The way
Brother Thomas explained it, God watched people continually, and not a detail escaped his notice or was omit-
ted from the record. As he went on talking I pictured
God sitting up in Heaven at a desk, adjusting his bi-
focals and looking down through the clouds at me all
day, itemizing my sins in a big leather-bound book:

1. Sassed his Grammaw.
2. Picked a fight with Hubert.
3.   "   " "   "   "
4.   "   " "   "   "
5. Threw Wilson's teddy bear over the smokehouse.
6. Played off sick to get out of work.
7. Ditto No. 2.

8. Claimed he had washed his feet for bedtime when he had only swiped them through the dew on the grass.

My sins were not only too numerous to mention; they were almost too numerous for one person to keep track of. God was so familiar with my sins by now that he probably sharpened a fresh pencil every morning when he saw me get out of bed.

Brother Thomas gave several hair-raising examples to show what happened to a person who thought he could sin and hide it from God. An hour later he wound up his sermon with the story of Cain and Abel. He told how Cain had fallen upon his brother Abel in the field and slain him when he thought God wasn't looking. But God *had been* looking. . . . "Yes, the Lord saw him, my brethren. . . . He marks the sparrow's fall. . . . PRAISE GOD! . . . AY-MEN."

Brother Thomas smacked his fist in his palm and described the awful scene where God had come down to earth and jumped on Cain for what he had done. The thunder had rolled, the lightning had flashed, the ground had trembled. Brother Thomas stomped on the platform and cracked his coattail like a whip, to show how angry God had been. And he finished by telling how Cain had been branded and chased off the face of the earth, and sent to Hell.

"Be careful how you treat your own brother, my friend . . ." He paused, and I thought he was going to look a hole through me. ". . . or God will send YOU to burn in everlasting Hell. AY-MEN. Let us pray."

All the way home, my conscience pinched me like my Sunday shoes. I felt much more sinful than Cain. I thought of the many, many times I had fallen upon my brother in the field. We argued about whose potato row had the most hills to dig, or about what looked like an unfair division of the weed pulling, as perhaps Cain and Abel had been doing. And then we fought. Of course I hadn't slain Hubert, but it wasn't because I didn't get as mad as Cain. Hubert was simply tougher than Abel.

Not three hours ago I had kicked my brother in the face and knocked him out of the sycamore tree. If God could mark a sparrow's fall, he had certainly marked Hubert's for he had hit the ground like a stick of stove wood. I assumed that God had jotted that down in the book and left a blank space underneath in case Hubert died from his injuries. Maybe Hubert had died in my absence, and maybe God was on the way down to earth to dispose of me as he had Cain. . . . Heat lightning blinked on and off in a cloud bank low in the west. I wondered if that meant anything. . . . I wished Old Nellie could trot a little faster through the hot darkness. I wanted to get home and make up with Hubert. I tried to think of something I could give him as a peace offering. The possession I treasured most was my gyroscope top. It was a wonderful top, a string-wound flywheel that whirled inside a couple of braced metal rings. It would spin anywhere, even on the edge of a water glass or the tip of a lead pencil. We had each bought a gyroscope top one summer out of our berry-picking money. Hubert's misbehaved one day and hopped off the snare cord we had stretched over the well.

At home I went straight to my secret hiding place in the dining-room closet and brought out the top. Grammaw had already come back from Schmidts'. She was sitting by a window, rocking Wilson to sleep. Devore had lain down across Mother's bed in the next room.

Mother asked Grammaw, "How is Hubert feeling by now?"

"Hubert?" Grammaw cried. She sprang out of her chair. "Merciful Father!" She sat down again as though her knees had received a shove from behind. "You mean to say he isn't with you?"

"No, we took Bruce, so they wouldn't fight," Mother said. "I'll bet Hubert fell asleep on the lounge."

Dad struck a match and looked on the screened porch. In the first flare of its yellow light I saw the empty lounge and the round, empty print of a head in the pillow. God had taken Hubert to Heaven. My repentance was too late. I stood and twirled the top between my fingers. My legs weakened as I thought of the punishment that was coming. That heat lightning in the west had been a sign, after all.

Dad said, "That's funny. I wonder where he could be."

Grammaw cried out, "He's gone. Hubert's lost."

Mother said, "No, he isn't lost, Ma. Maybe he went upstairs to bed."

"Not by himself in the dark, he wouldn't," Grammaw said. "Somebody stole him, that's what. Oh, I knew something dreadful would happen. I knew it when I saw that hoe in the house yesterday."

Grammaw had scolded Chod for his carelessness when, on Saturday morning, he'd come to the kitchen for a drink and forgotten to leave the strawberry hoe outdoors. An ax or a heavy garden tool accidentally carried into a dwelling was an omen of death or disaster. Now Hubert's disappearance verified it.

Hubert wasn't up in our bed. He wasn't downstairs. Mother and Dad and Grammaw looked in every room. They went around a second time. They ransacked the closets, looked under the beds, and behind the organ. They searched the cellar.

Grammaw cried, "Oh, why did I ever go to Barbara Schmidt's to visit and let a sneakin' band of gypsies come along and steal my grandson?"

"Ma, try not to carry on so," Mother begged her. "I don't think there've been any gypsies in the neighborhood. Hubert can't be far from the house. More than likely curled up asleep somewhere."

"We'll never find him alive," Grammaw sobbed.

Down in my heart I believed it to be true. But compared to my silent misery, Grammaw's loud distress was nothing. She was innocent of Hubert's loss, and she was only going by one of her omens. I was the guilty party. The authority of Genesis and Brother Thomas stared me in the face. God would probably be down any minute to settle things with me as he had with Cain. I wondered what awful tidings in the heavens would announce his arrival.

Dad woke Chod, and he came downstairs the fastest
we ever saw him during all the years he worked for Dad.
He lit a lantern and strode to the barn. Mother followed
Dad to the smokehouse, the woodshed, and the chicken
pens. Mother didn't act worried. I noticed, though, that
she didn't stop to examine a long tear made in her white
Sunday skirt by the jimsonweed burrs. Grammaw fluttered about the yard, wringing her hands and calling
Hubert in the flowerbeds.

Chod came back from the barn. He had searched the
buildings, including the berry shed by the road. There
was no trace of Hubert, he said. Dad set his lantern down.
He and Mother exchanged a long look without speaking.
I wished I hadn't seen them. It was a frightening,
wounded look.

"Hubert is somewhere on this place," Mother said.
"We're bound to find him if we keep hunting. Now
let's find out which one of us saw him last, and where
it was. Chod, you were at the barn when we went to
church. Hubert didn't come down there?"

"Nope."

"Ma, he was on the lounge when you went to Schmidts',
wasn't he?"

"And little did I think it was the last time I'd ever lay
eyes on him," Grammaw said. "I knew something bad
was takin' place. I could feel it in my bones all the time
I was at Barbara's."

Mother said, "Devore, when did you see him last?"

"Well, he got up off the lounge after he'd had his third
cup of tea. He went in the pantry and said he was going

to find where you hid the cake after supper. I don't know whether he found it or not. I was afraid it would get pitch dark before Grammaw came back, and so I took little Wilson and walked across the pasture to meet her."

"How long were you gone?"

"A good while. Grammaw was just coming down Schmidts' driveway when we met her."

"You didn't see Hubert after you came back?"

"No. I thought he was asleep on the lounge. It was dark out there, and I didn't go and look."

"And I thought the poor little thing was at church," Grammaw said. "Would to goodness he had a-been."

All this time I had been looking up toward Heaven for some portent. I wasn't surprised to see a jagged blaze of lightning shoot out of the sky in the southwest. A distant rumble of thunder jarred the ground.

"Merciful Father!" Grammaw wailed. "It's coming up a storm. And poor little Hubert out in it somewhere."

Dad and Chod held their lanterns behind them and examined the dark sky. Ugly clouds were piling up over the whole southwest.

Dad said, "Yes, I'm afraid we're going to have a shower. Chod, you jump on a horse and ride down and tell Mr. Barksdale and Walter to come up. Mother, I think you'd better telephone Schmidts' folks and Big Sam. Tell Big Sam to call Temples'. I'll go up in the wagon-shed loft once more and we'll search the spring hollow and then spread out through the woods."

It seemed like no time at all before a lantern light was bobbing across Big Sam's field, fading to a yellow spark in each blue lightning flash. Another showed up in the direction of Barksdales'. A tiny moving point of light appeared in the woods pasture toward Schmidts'. Not long afterward we heard the clatter of a wagon and saw the faint blob of a lantern along the lane from Uncle Constantine's.

I cringed as the lights from every direction drew near and closed in around me. All the people on Pleasant Ridge couldn't bring Hubert back. It would only mean a bigger audience when God came down to punish me. I wondered how Mother and Dad would feel, with one son taken away to Heaven and another sent down to Hell in front of all the neighbors. It sure would be lonesome for Grammaw, too, with both of us gone. I wet a finger and sizzled it against Dad's lantern globe, testing it for heat to see what Hell was going to be like.

John Schmidt and his hired hand came around the house through the backyard, followed by Barbara. Their good round Dutch faces were heavy with concern. Mr. Barksdale and his oldest son, Walter, arrived at a trot through the truck patch, with several coonhounds frisking and sniffing at the prospect of an all-night hunt. Fat Mrs. Barksdale waddled after them, puffing hard and poking her hand between her breasts to locate her thumpy heart. We could hear her crying out loud as she came into the yard. Molly Barksdale had thirteen children of her own, and yet she could weep at the thought of somebody else losing just one. The Temples' wagon jolted up the driveway, with Uncle Constantine and Matthew, Mark, Luke, and Miss Johanna looking as solemn as the mules that pulled it. Uncle Constantine said, " 'The Lord giveth and the Lord taketh away.' Job 1:21." Big Sam Johnson and Lettie and Truthful Thaddeus were the last. Lettie threw her arms around Mother's neck. Trouble had visited a family on Pleasant Ridge and, like always, the neighbors were ready to face it with them. They formed a little circle around Mother and Dad in the front yard. Mother seemed perfectly calm. She said, "The last we saw of Hubert was about seven o'clock. He was alone in the house after Devore took Wilson and started down toward the pasture. I don't suppose any of you folks have seen him since then?"

Nobody spoke for a moment. Then Thaddeus stepped forward. His red head shone like a beacon above the light of all the lanterns.

"Miz Bell," he said, "I saw him."

"Where?" Mother asked.

"Here."

Mother said, "I didn't know you were here after we went to church."

"Yes'm, I sure was," he said.

The men shifted their feet and stared uneasily at the ground. This was no time for Thaddeus to make up another one of his long-winded stories. The thunder sounded closer, and a light breeze rattled the leaves in the sycamore. But Thaddeus went on, "Mom sent me down with a basket of yellow pear tomatoes for you to make preserves."

Mother said, "I didn't see them."

"They're back there on your kitchen table. You can look if you don't believe me."

Lettie said, "Thaddeus, honey, you should have told somebody, not just left them there in the kitchen."

"I did tell somebody. I told Hubert. There wasn't anybody else in the house."

Mother asked, "Where was Hubert when you told him about the tomatoes?"

"He was in the pantry, cuttin' cake. He gave me a piece of it, and then went out to play."

"What happened next, Thaddeus?" Mother asked sharply. "Where did you play?"

"Around the well, under the box elder tree."

"Yes. Go on."

"And all at once I looked out in the chicken pen and a big black Devil with three horns was standin' in the jimsonweeds. His face was the color of your pink chicken house. He had a red-hot pokin' stick and—"

"Oh, Thaddeus," Mother said. "Please!"

Lettie spoke up. "Maybe you just imagined you saw it, honey." To Mother she said, "He must have thought he saw it. I don't think he'd lie about it. That wouldn't be Thaddeus. . . . Go ahead, honey. Tell Mrs. Bell what Hubert did when he saw the . . . the black Devil with three horns."

"Hubert didn't see it. Nobody saw it but me. I told Hubert how it looked. I told him it was liable to punch his eyes out with the red-hot pokin' stick. That's what my grandad said would happen to me if I started tellin' lies."

Mother said, "Everybody knows what a truthful boy you are, Thaddeus. Do you remember anything else?"

"Yes'm. Hubert said that must be the Old Scratch comin' to carry him off because him and Bruce had been fightin' on the Lord's Day. He said he'd kinda been expectin' him. He said he'd give me the rest of his piece of cake if I'd chase him away. Then he climbed up the box elder tree by the house and dropped down on the kitchen roof. He scrunched up and laid down behind the chimney where the roof's kinda flat. He told me not to let the Old Scratch know where he hid."

"What did you do then?"

"I stood there and ate the cake and watched the Devil. When he got pretty close I picked up some rocks and took out after him and—"

"How did Hubert get down from the roof after you chased the Devil away?"

"Well, it's a funny thing. I called him a couple of times and told him it was gone, but he didn't answer me. I happened to think that Mom had told me not to stay and play, so I left. But that same black Devil with three horns was cre-ee-pin' along the sassafras bushes and—"

Mother said, "Thank you, Thaddeus. That will do." She turned to Dad. "Do you suppose you ought to look on the kitchen roof?"

Dad shrugged his shoulders.

"Sometimes you find one grain of truth among the chaff. I'll see if there's a place up there where a boy could hide."

Chod brought a ladder from the woodshed. Dad hung a lantern on his arm and climbed up. His feet went clomping across the roof.

"Our lost boy is found!"

Grammaw took a new hitch in her weeping, but now it had a refreshing sound. Dad handed Hubert down from the roof. Chod reached up and got him. He was sound asleep. Mother undressed him, and he was put to bed without even being made to wake up and wash his his feet. Grammaw just took a wet washcloth and wiped some of the black off the bottoms, which showed more than anything else how much the family really prized Hubert.

The neighbors murmured good night and left.

All at once Mother collapsed in a chair and shut her eyes. Dry-looking little tears squeezed out and gathered on her cheeks. Her fingers cramped up in tight fists, and she shook like she had a chill. Dad and Grammaw rubbed her hands and arms. Chod ran to the cellar for a nip of the blackberry wine to revive her. Mother said she was all right, and we had better get some sleep. The clock had struck midnight.

Upstairs in our room I took off my Sunday clothes and blew out the lamp. Through the west window I saw Barksdales' lantern grow smaller and smaller as it went up the face of the hill. Through the south window I saw Schmidts' lantern light flicker in the woods pasture and lose itself among the trees. The accusing lights were gone. I felt less guilty. I had forgotten all about the storm. I saw that it had gone around. Far in the east I heard the faint rumble of retreating thunder. A bright shaving of new moon glowed in a silver blue sky. I knew that God was up there above it working late on his record book. He had changed his mind about sending me to Hell tonight. He had noticed my suffering and decided to place Hubert on the kitchen roof and rub out my sins just this one time. Lucky that Thaddeus was the biggest liar on Pleasant Ridge. At last God had found a use for the talent that everybody else ridiculed.

I said, "Now I lay me down to sleep." This time I didn't race through it and jump in bed during the last line. Before I said amen, I told God I was sorry about causing all that commotion in the neighborhood. I thanked him for his forgiveness and added that I hoped his pencil had a good eraser on it. And to show that my atonement was genuine, I rose early the next morning and gave Hubert my gyroscope top.

5

Swimming-Hole Reunion

CONCERNED AS SHE WAS OVER THE MORAL WELFARE OF Hubert and myself, Grammaw was equally solicitous of our physical well-being and, I might add, equally pessimistic about the end results of our behavior. From Grammaw's point of view, climbing a tree or riding a horse bareback was an open invitation to disaster, and as for swimming in water more than navel-deep without a life preserver, well, that was imposing too much of a chore upon the most alert of guardian angels. Grammaw, herself, was jooberous, as she called it, about entering any body of water larger than a half-filled tub.

And so Grammaw had a double reason for voicing her approval when she learned that Mother and Dad had forbidden us to go swimming in Mr. Schmidt's quarry pond on Sunday. For one day of the week, at least, she would not have to worry about death by drowning. And the rule conformed to her strict, old-fashioned Methodist belief that swimming on the Sabbath was sinful. Thus, she felt that some constructive action had been taken both toward saving our souls and protecting our bodies.

Without a doubt Hubert and Thaddeus and I were the three happiest boys on Pleasant Ridge when eventually we were allowed to go to the quarry. The place where we'd learned to swim was a small wet-weather pond in one corner of our barn lot. As a swimming hole, it left much to be desired. It was too near the road for privacy, and we had to swim with a pair of old, chopped-off overalls flapping about our legs. In dry weather the pond receded to a shallow pool. The water became dirty and stale, and after the sun shone on it all day it felt as warm as dog piddle. All you could say in favor of our pond was that it was wet.

By contrast, the quarry pond provided every convenience a boy could wish for in a swimming hole. It was located in the Schmidts' cow pasture, just below a steep hill that hid it from the public road. A smooth rock floor sloped down a short distance from the shallow end to a drop-off, and beyond that—so far as we could learn by minnowing down into it—the quarry had no bottom. A spring flowed from a deep cleft in the limestone and sliced up through the warm surface water like an icy knife. An old rock crusher stood near the deep end in water up to its underpinnings. A few planks pried from its bin and wedged into the framework at different levels gave us diving boards for all degrees of dare-taking.

Mr. Schmidt's cattle drank from a spring farther down in the pasture, and so after the rock road to Borden was finished and the quarry had been abandoned, Mr. Schmidt fenced it off for the pleasure of the neighborhood boys. Since there were no animals wading around the edges and dobbing the banks, the pond was always fresh and clean, which made it a fine source of water for the steam traction engine that operated the threshing machine. Mr. Schmidt generously allowed the pond to be used for that purpose, too. He built a gate so the water wagon could be backed inside and down the bank far enough for the hose of its little pitcher pump to reach the water. In threshing time the thirsty engine kept the driver going in and out of the quarry enclosure nearly all day, but after the machine pulled away from Pleasant Ridge in August, Mr. Schmidt nailed the gate shut, and then nobody entered the place except the boys who went swimming.

Dad made sure that Hubert and I could safely swim in deep water, and then he and Mother made the rules. The first was that we must never under any circumstances go there without asking permission. They wanted to keep track of us, Mother explained, so they could send for us if we were needed at home. And Grammaw added dourly that if we came up missing they would know whether to look for our bodies under the sycamore tree or start dragging the pond. The original rule about keeping the Sabbath holy was amended to include two parts. Part One: no swimming on Sunday. Part Two: no arguing about Part One.

The Johnsons were Methodists, too, and so the same restrictions governed Thaddeus.

Almost every weeknight during the summer, Thaddeus would come past our house and wait until Hubert and I finished our chores, and the three of us skinned out down the half-mile lane toward the quarry. Coming to the Schmidts' farm, we climbed a fence into their hay field and raced down the hill. We tore off our shirts and unbuckled our overall suspenders as we ran, and arrived at the pasture fence already stripped and ready for the water.

We could not be seen from the Schmidt house, for their yard was on a knoll high above the pond, and a rose of Sharon hedge along the side yard served as a screen. The shrubs were matted through a tall fence which separated the yard and the barn lot in back of it from the pasture. Anyone who wanted to look at our nakedness would have had to walk to the rear of the barn and climb on a stile at the corncrib, and we figured this was too much trouble for all they would see when they got there.

We folded our clothes and laid them by the fence under a sign that read:

MEAN BULL
STAY OUT.

This advice was not for us boys who came to the pond by way of the hay field. Mr. Schmidt knew that we were acquainted with the bull and would be able to take care of ourselves. He had nailed the warning on fenceposts at all places where a stranger might be tempted to take a shortcut across the meadow and not live to tell it.

Now, in case you are not personally acquainted with many bulls, they are as different as human beings in their dispositions. Some are peaceful and easygoing, some are big-mouthed bluffers, and others have murder in their hearts. Durham, the Schmidt bull, was one of the latter, and when he lowered his long sharp horns and charged, he meant business. He was not to be turned aside with rocks, as we did our own Jersey bull, Mr. Tyke. The only weapon he respected was a pitchfork, with the tines pointed at his face. Mr. Schmidt and his hired man carried a pitchfork whenever they stepped into the pasture, and so did the Schmidt boys when they crossed it to come down to the pond.

Durham had never actually gored anybody, but this was merely because all of his prospects had turned out under pressure to be swift runners and fancy high jumpers. Every time he chased a pedestrian out of the pasture, Barbara Schmidt exclaimed, in the combination of broken English and High German she used in moments of excitement, "John, I vant you to rid yourself of dat bull before he hooks a person to death vunce." But even though Durham hated people, he had a nice way with the milk cows, and John kept him.

Durham despised young boys more than other kinds of people, for he considered them his worst intruders, and he held a special grudge against Hubert and Thaddeus and me. We annoyed him more regularly, and perhaps worse, than any of the other boys who swam in the pond. Every evening about sunset he planted his enormous red and white spotted bulk at the fence and waited for us to run down through the hay field, meanwhile uttering angry remarks to himself, like Uncle Constantine quoting scripture.

A strip of pasture some fifty yards wide lay between

the hay field fence and the quarry enclosure. Of course we had to cross this in order to reach the swimming hole. To do this, one of us boys would wrench a small limb from a dead apple tree nearby, and lean across the fence and break it over the bull's head. Then we'd throw the butt end down in the pasture a ways, and when Durham turned and started goring the stick to splinters, we'd slip over the fence and dart to the quarry.

We found it to our advantage to undress in the hay field first and run naked across the strip of ground that Durham guarded. A pair of overalls had too many seams and loose pockets that might catch on the upper strand of barbed wire. With a savage bull fanning your heels, you can't afford to spend much time hung up on a fence.

In our hurry to get into the water as soon as possible, we usually forgot to take off our hats until we were inside the quarry. In fact, it wasn't at all uncommon to see a stark naked boy walk out on the diving board for his first plunge, and then remember that he was still wearing his hat. It was a natural oversight. Every man and boy on Pleasant Ridge wore his light straw hat so continually from spring thaw till autumn frost that he was no more conscious of it than he was of his hair. All the boys except Thaddeus chose pretty much the same models: turned up in back and down in front and differing only as to the color of the band or the shape of the dents in the crown. But Thaddeus liked to be well-shaded, even to the ends of his turned-up toes, and he always wore a perfectly round, stiff-brimmed curiosity that would crowd a buggy wheel for size. We could never find out where he got them, for no store in Borden carried such out-landish headgear. Anyhow, we all agreed that Thaddeus, without the rest of his clothes, didn't resemble a boy wearing a straw hat as much as he did a toadstool mounted on short legs.

Getting back to Durham, he would notice that we had played the same old trick on him and slipped into the quarry while his back was turned. He bellowed like a maniac and lunged at the fence while inside it we splashed water and booed at him from the diving boards. (Mr. Schmidt used a woven wire fencing, guaranteed bull-proof.) Whenever Durham began to simmer down, one of the boys would run up the bank and shake a straw hat against the fence and stoke him up again. This went on till dark, when Mr. Schmidt's hired hand rode a horse down to the quarry and drove Durham to the stable for the night.

This went on practically every Sunday afternoon, too, but that was without Hubert and Thaddeus and me. Most of the boys we played with were Catholics, and they were allowed more freedom. On hot Sunday after-noons, during the long idle gap between dinner and supper, we thought of that cool, deep water in the quarry, and it exerted a pull on our sweating flesh like a magnet attracting horseshoe nails.

Hubert and I tried to obey our parents and shun all thought of evil. So did Truthful Thaddeus, occasionally. But at times it was easy to forget God's big black record book that Brother Thomas had so eloquently described, even easier to assume that at this particular moment

God might be occupied with recording the similar sins of other boys we knew. It was hard enough when we were separated, but let the three of us be together, and temptations buzzed around us like gnats over a cider barrel. They bothered us worse than usual one hot Sunday afternoon in July when we were in our woods pasture building a dam across the creek. One stung Thaddeus first. He pulled off his straw hat and wiped his freckled forehead.

"Be a good day to go swimming."

Hubert and I both spoke at once: "Mother wouldn't let us, and neither would yours."

Hubert took his hands out of the bucket of loblolly he was stirring up for mortar and let the creek water riffle through his fingers. He said, "Just for fun, let's go back to the house and ask Mother one more time."

Thaddeus said, "Let's don't and say we did. Your mom is like mine—awful headstrong." He looked up at the blazing sky. "Besides, we could go—we *could* go—for just a minute and they wouldn't either one have to find it out."

"Somebody would tattle on us," Hubert reminded him. "That's for sure."

"The only person that'd tattle would be Mrs. Schmidt. She knows our women folks are all Methodists. We could be real quiet, though, and she wouldn't know we were there. They can't see us from the house. All we'd have to do'd be watch the sun and slip back here in time for our hair to dry before we went home."

I had the next idea: "If we went to the house and told

Mother we wanted to go swimming, you know what I'd
say? I'd say, 'Mother, just why is it any more sinful to
take off our overalls and lay down in Mr. Schmidt's pond
than it is to roll them up to our knees and stand in our
crick?' "

Hubert said, "I'd like to see her get around that argument. She'd say to Grammaw, 'Why *is* it any more sinful,
Ma?' And Grammaw couldn't think of any reason why,
and she'd say, 'Lulie, I never had looked at it that way.
It's as broad as it is long. Why don't you let 'em go to the
pond?' And Mother would say, 'Run along, boys, and
swim all afternoon.' And Grammaw would say, 'Don't
you dare tease that bull or I'll switch the daylights out of
you.' And then we could swim and tease the bull till
supper time."

"That's exactly the way it'd turn out," Thaddeus said.
"Whew, that sun's awful hot, and it's a long ways back
to your house. It's closer than that to the quarry. About
a good rock throw from the far edge of that cornfield. We
could be in the water in less time that it'd take us to go
and ask your folks."

Hubert and I agreed with Thaddeus. What a short,
easy route it would be, if only we had the nerve to take
it. . . . Out of the woods pasture into our cornfield.
. . . We could hunch over, and the tall rustling stalks
would hide us as we sneaked through. . . . At the road
we must stop and look up and down both ways to see if
the coast was clear. . . . Then a hop, skip, and a jump
across the warm velvet dust in the wheel tracks. . . .
And over the fence into Mr. Schmidt's hay field. . . .

Quick! . . . Now a short hard run down the hill and we would be there. . . .

The still small voices of conscience spoke up and tried to dissuade us. They were pretty faint and they were a little late, besides, for by the time they had made themselves clearly understood Hubert and Thaddeus and I were going down through Mr. Schmidt's hay field like three runaway mules, and half-stripped.

The pond was deserted. Durham was grazing on the far side of the quarry with his back turned. The sun was still high in the sky, and so Durham didn't expect any boys for several hours yet. In a matter of seconds we shed the rest of our clothes and crossed the narrow strip of pasture. Hubert and I climbed the quarry fence; Thaddeus was bringing up the rear. Durham still hadn't heard us when Hubert and I slipped around to the other side of the pond. We stooped down in the tall hog weeds. Hubert called out from our hiding place: "Moo-oo-ooooo, you old spotted windbag."

Durham recognized Hubert's voice or perhaps he recalled the name. He came running, head high and tail stiffened, reaching out in long-legged strides like a pacing horse. We crouched down until he began to sniff the wire fence. Then we jumped up and mooed. Durham let out a bellow that shook the rock crusher. We could see clear down in his pink, slippery gullet. We took off our straw hats and flapped them against the fence. We had often wondered how much pressure a mean bull could build up inside before he exploded. This afternoon would be a good time to find out.

We turned to see what was keeping Thaddeus. He stood on one leg outside the enclosure, tweezing a briar out of his foot.

"Come on, Thaddeus," Hubert called. 'We've got him mad enough to bust already."

Behind us a board cracked. Hubert and I spun around and found ourselves staring right into Durham's bloodshot eyes. His flat red face looked as broad as the side of a barn. His head and shoulders were inside the gate. We hadn't remembered to examine it. The thought flashed through my mind that the water-wagon driver in his haste on Saturday afternoon had merely pulled it shut and failed to put up the four-by-four bars that braced it.

Durham shouldered the gate aside and came at us. His breath was hot on our backs as we went headlong over the bank. We h:t belly-whopper-style. Purely by luck, we struck water and not a limestone slab.

Durham was everywhere at once. If we swam toward a bank, he was there, horning the dirt and waiting. If we headed for the rock crusher, he was there, butting the underpinnings. He had us where he had always wanted us. He spotted our straw hats where we had dropped them in the hog weeds. He gave mine a sideswipe as he passed in a gallop, and speared it like a marshmallow on a fork. He turned on Hubert's and in a minute reduced both of ours to one small pile of chaff.

Thaddeus stood like a one-legged dummy outside the fence, forgetting to set down the foot with the briar in it. His mouth hung open.

In the deep end of the pond, I spewed out a mouthful of water and chattered, "Thaddeus, tell Mr. Schmidt! Tell Mr. Schmidt to bring a pitchfork and drive him away. Hurry, Thaddeus! We can't tread water much longer."

Thaddeus quickly circled the quarry and ran a few steps toward the house. He cupped his hands to his mouth and hollered, "Mr. Schmidt! Oh, Mr. Schmidt!"

No answer. He ran farther up the hill. This time he really screamed: "Mr. Schmidt! Come down here quick! The bull's got Bruce and Hubert cornered."

Nobody could see us through the hedge. Not a thing moved in the barn lot. I stretched my neck and looked at the corncrib. Oh, why didn't Mr. Schmidt show up at the stile with a pitchfork in his hand? Where *was* everybody?

"Thaddeus!" Hubert shouted. "Watch out for the bull. Here he comes."

In a flash, Durham was out through the broken gate and into the pasture. Thaddeus whirled around. He found his retreat blocked.

The bull stopped bellowing. He put his head down and examined Thaddeus. Everything was dead silent, except for the sound of Durham's hard breathing. He snorted, and two puffs of dust rose under his nostrils.

Thaddeus stepped to one side, figuring that maybe he could dodge the bull and make a dash for the pond. Durham took a step forward. Thaddeus backed up one. Thaddeus stepped to the other side. Durham took another step forward. Thaddeus backed up another one. Durham's lowered head swept back and forth, covering every movement.

Thaddeus could see that this kind of a zigzag was simply working him farther and farther away from the pond. In all other directions there was only a wide stretch of open meadow. Not even a thorn tree to climb. Thaddeus risked a quick look over his shoulder.

The nearest refuge was the yard fence on the hilltop. Getting through the matted rose of Sharon hedge would be a tedious business, and Thaddeus knew he would be pressed for time, even if he reached it ahead of the bull. The stile at the corner of the corncrib would be easy to clear, but a lot of ground lay between him and the stile, all of it upgrade. He didn't have much time to choose.

The bull charged.

Thaddeus took a few quick steps toward the hedge. Then, as though changing his mind, he turned and cut up the long slope toward the corncrib. The bull roared after him, horns low and straight out in front, tail high and straight out behind.

Hubert and I pulled ourselves out of the water and clung to the rock crusher. I tightened every muscle in my body as I tried to send a part of their strength out across space and into Thaddeus's flying legs. The bull seemed to be gaining. I heard Hubert pleading, "Go-Thaddeus-go."

The last we saw of him, Thaddeus was still going. Then we heard a thud and a hard grunt. It looked like they were down on the ground. A cloud of dust boiled up and hid everything. We knew that Thaddeus was still alive. We heard him scream, "Help! Help! Mr. Schmidt, help." Then silence.

Mr. Schmidt was awhile getting there. He hadn't heard Thaddeus calling from the pond because of the noise in his backyard. It was the Sunday of the Schmidt family's annual reunion and basket dinner. They had met this time with John and Barbara. All of John's folks were there: Great-grandpa Schmidt, who had the trembles and walked with a cane; Father Paul Schmidt from the Seminary; Miss Marie, Barbara's older sister who clerked in a department store in Town; John's aunts and uncles; his three married sisters and four brothers and their families, on down to the newest diapered grandchild.

The Schmidts had eaten their family-reunion dinner at long tables spread in the cool shade of the poplar trees in the backyard. The men were sitting around in groups afterward, telling jokes and laughing over their elderberry wine. The women were clearing up the dishes, exchanging cake recipes, and yelling at the kids to play their game of hide-and-go-seek without quite so much screaming.

John heard the bull carrying on down in the meadow somewhere. He hardly gave it a thought. He knew Durham's disposition. A bellow from the direction of the pond was no more out of the ordinary than a frog's croak.

The bellowing went on, though, and finally Miss Marie said, "John, isn't that a mister-cow mooing down in the pasture?"

"Yes, that's Durham. He moos a good deal of the time."

Father Paul said, "He seems to be angry about something."

John said, "There must be some kids in the pond. I think I heard boys yelling a minute ago."

Great-grandpa Schmidt spoke up, "They're teasin' him, that's what. Ought to put a stop to it."

Barbara said, "If it's Thaddeus Johnson and dem Bell boys, dere mudders don't allow dem in de pond on Sunday. It's against dere religion. John, go out by de corncrib and look down in de pasture vunce."

"Oh, let them alone, Barbara. Durham will calm down after a while."

Instead of calming down, he grew more excited. They could hardly talk for the noise. The smaller kids tried to pry an opening in the hedge and peep into the pasture. The men looked restless. Miss Marie said, "Barbara, I'm scared. I think I'll go in the house."

Barbara insisted, "John, something is ailing dat bull. He never gets so mad as dat yet."

Julius, the oldest Schmidt boy, said, "He's more than just mad this time. Listen, Dad. He's chasing somebody. It sounds like they're headed this way."

The ear-splitting roars were coming up the slope, closer and closer.

"I'll get a pitchfork," John cried, upsetting several chairs on his way to the barnyard gate.

"Careful he don't hook you, John," yelled Barbara.

From the pasture came a crashing noise. Then a hard grunt.

"Help! Help! Mr. Schmidt, help!"

"The bull's got him down!"

Father Paul flew after John and the women ran, too. Great-grandpa Schmidt skipped after them, missing every other stroke with his cane. They all raced along the hedge. Barbara panted, "Time and again I tell John to get rid of dat bull. But no, he vaits too long."

Just then what looked like a streak of lightning in a straw hat flashed over the stile and came around the corncrib.

Truthful Thaddeus!

What nobody found out for some time was that the bull had lost the race before Thaddeus reached the fence. Durham twisted his foot on a loose rock and turned a somersault in the dust at Thaddeus's heels. It smashed the wind out of him, but Thaddeus heard that terrible grunt and he thought he was a goner. He screamed for help and spurted ahead. He covered the last few rods of the field and crossed the stile—four steps up and four steps down—like he was running over a few boards laid flat on the ground. His speed carried him around the corncrib before he could shut it off, and he went through the family reunion like a runaway horse splitting a flock of chicken hens. Finally he pulled up face to face with Mrs. Schmidt.

Thaddeus prided himself on his cool head in emergencies, and of course it would take more than a narrow escape from a death-dealing bull to catch him without an innocent reason for passing the swimming hole on Sunday.

"Mrs. Schmidt," he said politely, forgetting for a moment that he was stark naked except for his toadstool hat, "Mom sent me down to ask if she could borrow a spool of number-fifty white thread."

6

A Cat Named Joseph

ALTHOUGH GRAMMAW'S LIFE ON THE FARM WAS OFTEN punctuated by moments of jarring discord, most of them created by Hubert and me, there was one area in which all three of us enjoyed perfect harmony. Grammaw shared our love for cats. In fact, she was so fond of them that for their benefit she would sometimes make certain departures from her orderly manner of keeping house, an indulgence she never granted Hubert and me. Voluntarily, that is. She pinned the lace curtains up beyond jumping distance, moved the bric-a-brac to safe places, and let the kittens romp through the house. And so it was not surprising when Grammaw joined us in defense of an unwanted kitten that came one winter night to join the family.

A cold February rain was drumming gently on the roof and sluicing down the windowpanes. The night wind sighed in the dining-room chimney. We sat in a close half circle about the fireplace and toasted our shins in the glow of red-hot hickory coals. Mother was shaking the long-handled corn popper over the coals to encourage the last fragrant grain to explode. It was the kind of night to feel thankful for warm shelter and to think of the livestock warmly bedded down for the night. Grammaw's swift knitting needles paused.

She said, "Did I hear a cat meow?"

Dad said, "No cat in its right mind would venture out on a night like this. Probably a wet sycamore limb scraping the weather boarding."

Grammaw resumed her knitting. "There!" she said, after a moment. "Don't you hear it? I know that's a kitten."

She took a lamp and went to the kitchen door. Peering down under the shade of her hand, she saw a dark little animal not much larger than a person's hand huddled in the shelter of the lower step. Two points of green fire reflected the light of her lamp.

"Mew," the animal said in a weak voice.

"Oh, you poor little critter," Grammaw said. "Where'd you come from?"

A strange kitten climbed up the steps and dragged itself across the threshold. It crept into the dining room, trailing water and footprints over the linoleum. It sat down on the hearth, tilted a mud-spattered face upward, and examined first one and then another of us as if choosing with care the person it intended to adopt. Feeling the warmth of a smooth brick under its body, it tuned up and tried a small purr; but it was shivering from head to foot and all it achieved was a bit of feeble, irregular rattle. It applied a sliver of red tongue to a front paw and set about cleaning up. Hubert and I took a gunnysack and wiped it dry. In doing so, we found out that it was a male cat, and we saw that its fur was not black, but an odd mixture of spots.

I said, "We'll have to name him Joseph, for his coat of many colors."

Hubert said, "Maybe he was his father's favorite and his brethren sold him into bondage and he ran away and came here."

Dad looked up from his *Farmer's Guide*. "Well, you can tell Joseph to keep right on traveling till he comes to Egypt. You have enough cats around here now to stock a dozen farms, and you're not going to take in another one."

Dad was like most of the farmers on Pleasant Ridge in his feeling for farm animals. He used up the greatest part of his love on the horses, currying and brushing them every morning as carefully as he combed his hair. What was left of his affection dwindled down through the cows, hogs, and chickens, and petered out before it reached the cats. He seemed to take it as a sort of rebuke to his own manliness that his sons had inherited their grandmother's affection for cats; though why it should be feminine to love a cat, and masculine to love a dog, was something I never did hear explained.

I used to tell Dad about Mark Twain and his fondness for cats. I had read somewhere that when he leased a summer home in the country he often went to a farm close by and rented several cats to keep him company during his vacation. In his city home he would send the butler out for his favorite kittens every evening, and he would get down on the library floor and romp with them by the hour. Of course, the example of Mark Twain would never convince a farmer like Dad that a real he-man sometimes played with cats. After all, Mark Twain only sat around and wrote books. He didn't farm.

But, for all of his gruff talk, Dad was too humane to throw a tiny animal out in the cold rain. He said, "You can fix a warm place in the barn tonight. But *tomorrow* you'll have to get rid of him."

Hubert and I bundled up in coats and overshoes and braved the path to the barn in the peppering rain. Hubert took the lantern, and I carried Joseph. He sniffed and rooted in the wrinkles of my coat sleeve, hunting desperately for nourishment. He felt as thin and flat as an empty sausage casing. Unfortunately, Joseph had arrived at the only time in our memory when we didn't have a mother cat who could sneak him into her brood and feed him.

Hubert said, "Give him to me and bring the lantern down in the cow stable. I'll see if Daisy's got any milk left."

It was only a few hours since the cows had been milked. Daisy's udder was limp, but she had enough strippings to make a stream. Hubert took a teat in his right hand and held the kitten with his left. He squeezed out a thin jet and it hit Joseph's mouth. Joseph snapped at the milk and gulped it down like a long white thread, until his mouth was at the end of the teat. He hooked his claws on Hubert's wrist for support and went to nursing like a noisy newborn calf. Of course, he was not actually sucking the teat—Hubert was pressing the milk out of it—but Joseph believed he was nursing, and Daisy must have thought so, too. Daisy mooed and, turning her head against the stanchion, she watched the feeding of her unexpected baby with no little surprise.

Hubert handed Joseph back to me. His belly was pooched out as tight and round as a tick. He blinked at the lantern, hiccuped, and fell asleep in my hands.

We made him a nest in a bushel basket half-full of hay and, as his fur was still damp, we spread a horse blanket over the top. As we returned to the house we made plans to hide him from Dad, by the usual neat trick of turning him loose among the other cats.

A great many kittens came uninvited to our place. The neighbors knew that Hubert and I were cat fanciers from away back, and so instead of drowning their surplus kittens they sacked them up on a dark night and dumped them out near our driveway. The ones who survived passing buggy wheels, varmints, and bad weather crawled into the barn lot. Hubert and I doctored and fed them and, after a little fur-pulling here and there, our own big cat family agreed to take them in. Dad disliked them all too much to notice two or three new faces around the barn. He slapped them out of the milk buckets and spluttered, "Something's got to be done about these nasty cats by *tomorrow*," under the impression that he was complaining about the same old bunch.

Joseph was still asleep next morning when we uncovered his basket. He woke up, stretched, split his face in a pink yawn, and hopped out on the barn floor, asking if breakfast was ready. His fur was now fluffy dry, and we had our first chance to examine his coloring. Hubert said the people in the cat factory who put the spots on him must have lost their pattern. They had evidently taken the remnants of their soft, heavier quality furs—black, yellow, white, gray, maltese, and tiger—slapped them over his frame in a dim light, and then screwed on a stump of a tail originally meant for a plain yellow kitten. Around his waist he wore a wide band of pure white, like an over-size vest split between the shoulder blades and buttoned wrong in front.

We tanked him up again on Daisy's warm strippings and hid his basket in back of the bran box out of Dad's way until we could think of a new scheme. Passing Joseph off among a bunch of ordinary spotted and striped cats would be like hiding a geranium in Grammaw's violet bed. We hurried home from school that afternoon and ran to the barn. The basket was empty.

We went through the barn with a lantern, hunting in all the dark niches around the feed bins and mangers where a kitten might have crawled away and fallen asleep. No Joseph. Hubert said, "I'll bet you a quarter Dad carried him off."

"No, I haven't seen him," Dad said. "And I don't want to see him. Good riddance. Go and get the buckets. It's time to milk."

I went into the stable through the door at the end where Daisy stood. Looking down at the straw bedding, I saw what appeared to be a small parcel of calico scraps between the cow's hind feet. Joseph was waiting for supper. Dad came in before we finished feeding him. He said, "Is that the kitten you were hunting? And what the dickens is going on there? Good Lord! Hurry up about it and take that hit-and-miss animal out of the stable. Makes me dizzy to look at it. Tomorrow's Saturday, don't forget, and you'll have to find a home for that cat. It's the last time I'm going to tell you."

Grammaw came to our aid. "William," she said as we sat around the fireplace after supper, "if I was you I'd think twice before I made the boys get shut of that kitten."

"Why so?"

"Something tells me he was sent as an omen."

"An omen of more kittens in the future, if I know anything about tomcats. What makes you think it's an omen?"

"The odd way he's marked, and all. I never saw a kitten like him before."

"Or behind either. Marked! You said it. His mother must have been scared by a rag rug."

Grammaw ignored this thrust at another one of her superstitions. "And the way he came a-meowin' at the door on a stormy night. The little bugger couldn't have found it all by himself. I believe that kitten was sent to this place for a purpose we don't know about."

Dad said, "But why a kitten? The boys have two cats for every mouse around the place. You can't walk through the yard, you can't step in the barn without a whole Coxey's Army of cats marching across your path. They drink enough milk every day to fatten several hogs."

Grammaw said, "If they're as thick as all that, William, one little feller the size of a corncob won't break you up."

Mother said, "Besides, you know he would starve if you took him off somewhere and the boys and Daisy couldn't feed him. I don't see why you want to raise such a racket over one small animal."

"Who's raising a racket, for heaven's sakes?" Dad shouted. "I didn't know the whole family was going to jump on me. All right, then, they can keep it till it's big enough to wean. But no longer. That's what gets me, to think of two strolloping big boys of mine helping a half-pint kitten suck a cow. Great Scott! I never heard of such nonsense."

Mother said, "I suppose you have forgotten those six little spotted pigs the old white sow wouldn't claim, and we raised them on a bottle. Nobody made fun of you when you took a hungry pig on your lap and stuck a nipple in its mouth."

"But a *pig*, yes! A pig grows into something. You know what that litter of shoats brought on the market?"

Grammaw's eyes flashed, but she spoke quietly: "What's fit to do for money is fit to do for love."

Eventually, Dad concluded that Grammaw was right about Joseph being sent to our house for a reason. But first that cat was to try Dad's patience in a great many ways.

Hubert and I weaned him from Daisy before he was ready. Joseph formed a bad feeding habit as he grew stronger, and Daisy kicked about it. The way a hungry calf orders its mother to give her milk down is to butt his head against her udder while he is nursing (and often it's such a savage butt you wonder that he doesn't boost her hind feet off the ground). Daisy had suckled five or six calves of her own, and she was used to their kind of priming. Instead of butting her when he wanted a heavier flow of milk, this strange little foster son opened up a fistful of pinpoint claws and ripped down the side of her udder. Having her teats clawed up into chipped beef twice a day upset Daisy. Not that you could blame her. She finally got so provoked, and so sore, that she would whale away and kick the milking stool out from anybody —including Dad—who sat down and took hold of her.

Dad used a box of Cloverine salve and all of his self-control before Daisy's udder and her disposition were both healed to the place where she would stand and let herself be milked without a rope hobble on her back legs. Meanwhile, Hubert and I taught Joseph to drink from a saucer. He learned—perhaps faster than most kittens— that when we dipped his nose into the milk he was supposed to lap it up from the surface, not wade into the dish and sit down. He graduated, and soon he was fighting for his place around the feeding pad and holding his own among all the old veteran cats.

By this time he was a healthy, active kitten, and well-filled out. Crouched on the floor with all four legs tucked under him, he might easily have been mistaken for one of the padded brickbats that Grammaw covered with bright patchwork and used around the house as door-stops. The combination of a brindle cow and a boy in overalls was the only mother Joseph had ever known. He followed us everywhere to our chores. He batted at the cobs when we shelled corn; he investigated crawdads in the horse trough while we caught spring water; he scurried through the weeds and tall grass as far as the back apple orchard, ready to jump and nail down every windfall apple we reached for.

Dad scowled and said every day after Joseph was weaned that he "was going to get rid of that nasty kitten." It was easier for Dad to threaten to dispose of a cat tomorrow than it was to come right out and do it today. So Joseph stayed at our house—hated, loved, and living on borrowed time. He had committed the sin of not being born a colt or a pig.

Ordinarily, Joseph shunned the cool ground under the hollyhocks where the other kittens napped in summertime. He took as his favorite snoozing place an old leather easy chair on the screened porch that the rest of us reserved for Dad's use. Joseph would jump up to its scabby seat, roll over in the hollow between the cushion and the armrest, and sleep—flat on his back with all four feet drawn up together on his white vest. Dad found him there nearly every time he wanted the chair. He took Joseph by the scruff of the neck and tossed him out on the grass, always making the same parting threat: "You sneaking little devil. I'll slap you to sleep the next time I catch you in my chair."

This happened almost every morning after Dad came back from feeding the stock and sat down on the porch to wait for breakfast. Grammaw had heard him make this same angry promise several times a day for a long while. One morning she asked in a kind of mocking voice, "William, why didn't you do it while you had him in your hands?"

"Hrrrmph," Dad answered. "You wait and see."

A few hours later, Dad went into the separator house and noticed that Hubert and I had failed to carry the morning's cream to the cellar after we separated the milk. He blamed this forgetfulness on the cats. He said that feeding them took so much of our time that we couldn't keep our minds on our work.

Their breakfast came the first thing after the separating. We took the buckets of warm skim milk and set them on the ground and called. Cats popped up and sped across the yard from every direction. They stood with their front feet on a bucket rim and lapped down through the foam, which had been raised up in a stiff mound by the force of the milk pouring from the separator spout. After they finished drinking, Hubert and I fed the skim milk to the hogs and then—if we could remember—we carried the cream to the cellar. Cream must be cooled quickly if you want good butter. And a lot of our income depended on the top-notch butter that Mother churned for the McKinley Hotel in Borden. Dad had cautioned us many times. But here, for the third time in three days, he discovered the cream still sitting in the hot separator house at going-on-ten in the morning.

Dad picked up the bucket and, furiously, started to the cellar. It did not improve his disposition when a sliver of gravel wedged under the open door and denied him the pleasure of slamming it behind him. He set the bucket on the ground and stooped down to dislodge the gravel.

Joseph was sitting on a gatepost nearby, and seeing a bucket appear out of the separator house with a thick pile of foam on top, he misunderstood it for an extra meal call. He made a flying leap from the post. This time there were no big cats to shove him aside. Dad was reaching down to pick up the bucket when a speckled cannonball with a short yellow fuse in back hurtled across the grass out of control and plopped heels over head into the cream.

"Four gallons. *Only* four gallons," Dad said, draining the bucket in a hog trough. "The next time he does that I won't fish him out. I'll drown him in good, rich, high-priced cream."

A sopping wet and badly scared little Joseph slunk off and joined a group of older kittens who were sitting on the back steps, and when Grammaw opened the door to go out and feed the dog, he slipped into the kitchen. In Grammaw's absence, Dad went to the kitchen for a drink. The cracked blue willow cereal dish that Grammaw used for feeding the cats their table scraps was sitting on the floor where Dad had to step around it. And over it, like a long-whiskered cream puff, squatted little Joseph, wearing on his face the wide-eyed, thoughtful expression of a child breaking in his first chamber pot. He had no brothers to share his guilt. Poor Joseph. Dad mopped out the cereal dish with him, and he did so thorough a job that Joseph could never again face a piece of blue willow ware without stopping to scrub his nose.

At two o'clock the same afternoon, the stiff-collared dude who sat in the leather easy chair on the screened porch bore no resemblance to the dirt farmer Dad had been that morning. The reason for the big change was Nancy Brock's wedding. The Brocks counted themselves among the Upper Tens, and they were putting on style—with printed invitations, store-bought ice cream, and a preacher from Town.

Dad had hitched Old Nellie to the buggy and driven to the house before he bathed and dressed. He was particular about not having a white horse hair or a trace of stable odor on his new blue serge suit. He flicked an imaginary speck of lint from his sleeve, fingered his necktie and the starched white bosom of his shirt, and called to ask Mother how much longer it was going to take her, for heaven's sakes, to pin one hat on her head. "We'll be late for the wedding march," he said.

"I'm coming right away," Mother called back from the downstairs bedroom.

Her answer was cut short by a crash in the dining room, followed by a thud, easily recognized as four soft paws hitting the floor. We heard the flapping of paper and at the same time a loud volley of popgun *sptt's* that meant a kitten in a fighting mood. The noise passed into the bedroom. Mother burst into laughter and the odd flapping sound seemed to go faster.

Sptt . . . (flap) . . . sptt . . . (flap-flap).

Joseph tore out of the sitting room and came down the hall, bristled up, with his ears laid flat. Stuck tight to his hind end and back legs was a big sheet of tanglefoot fly paper, which he had absentmindedly sat down upon. Blowing and spitting and kicking high up behind to loosen the thick, gum-sticky paper, he crossed the porch at a swift lopsided gallop, did a quick handstand, paper and all, and disappeared like fury through the dining-room door.

The sight really would have cracked up even Uncle Constantine. It struck Dad as the funniest thing he had ever seen. He let out a roar and bent over with his hands to his sides. "Ho-ho, ha-ha," he laughed. "Don't stop him. Let him make another round." He pulled out a handkerchief to wipe his eyes.

Joseph came down the hall on his second lap. He was now too scared and mad to deal with his tormentor alone. He needed help. He made a flying leap to one side and landed with a crush of tanglefoot streamers in Dad's lap. His fur still bore the fragrance of his housebreaking ordeal.

Dad took a wet washcloth and a sharp knife and cleaned the tanglefoot from his new suit. The crease in his trousers was ruined. He said he would lower the buggy top and let the sun dry the spots on the way to Brocks'. Mother examined him and said, "You really sopped them, didn't you? I doubt if that serge dries out before we get there." Her nose wrinkled. "William, you'll have to change your clothes. Going to the wedding in wet pants is bad enough, but what will people think if they come close enough to smell you? Phew!"

Dad went to put on his old baggy-kneed gray suit, saying, "One of these times I'm going to kill that nasty kitten with one blow."

The memory of the whole aggravating day was sticking him like a cockle burr when he went to the screened porch at dusk after the evening's chores were done. He was growling, "I'd better not find that little stinker in my chair tonight. For *if I do—*"

Sure enough, there between the cushion and the armrest lay the dark rounded shape that was so hateful and so familiar. "I've had enough out of you for one day," Dad shouted. "Scat out of here, you dirty shyster. *Scat.*" He drew back a strong right arm and slapped his old felt hat clear across the porch.

Joseph had had a hard day, too. He was asleep under the hollyhocks with some of his own people.

After Joseph reached his majority and began to go out courting, Dad could no longer call him "that nasty kitten." From then on, he was never anything but "that ornery tomcat." Though he had outgrown all the innocent ways of his kittenhood, his affection for us boys never waned. He would choose one of our laps, then climb up and flatten himself on a shirtfront so that he could look into our eyes. He was now a fourteen-pound enlargement of the tiny kitten Grammaw had found on the doorstep less than a year and a half ago. His face was round and puffy and crisscrossed with battle scars, his jowls heavy, and he had a protruding lower lip that was bright pink and made him look like the villain in a cartoon. But his topaz eyes glittered with adoration, his mouth would water, and he filled the room with a thundering purr of contentment. And we loved Joseph all the more because he was a pariah elsewhere.

I have to admit that after Joseph came into the full bloom of his power he justified his reputation as a hell-raiser in the neighborhood. He was not content to be the boss in our own big family of cats. His ambition was to be head man among all the pussycats on Pleasant Ridge. I doubt if a tomcat in Clark County faced rougher competition, or more of it. It cost Joseph nearly all of his night's rest, his fine reputation with the neighbors, and some good-sized patches of his fur, but he stayed on top of the heap.

Joseph continued to spend a great deal of time each day in Dad's old leather chair. He dressed last night's wounds and mended the slits in his ears and then turned over and slept. Usually, when Dad went to the chair he found him sprawled on his back, snoring, his whiskers twitching, and both hind feet digging the bowels out of some rival who disturbed his dreams. Dad yanked him out—not by the scruff of the neck anymore, for his dangling carcass made a good double handful—and flung him outdoors, saying, "Been nighthawking again, have you? You ornery tomcat."

Actually, Joseph was no more to blame for traipsing over the countryside than Chester, our registered Poland China boar hog. But neither Dad nor any other farmer in the neighborhood could be convinced of that fact. Chester had the advantage of being needed.

He was the only male hog on Pleasant Ridge, and such a fine animal that all the farmers considered his services worth every penny of the one-dollar breeding fee Dad charged them. The odd thing about Chester was that he knew when one of his wives was due to pay him a visit. Instead of waiting until she could be loaded into a farm wagon and hauled to our place, he went to call on her, although how he could tell the exact date without a calendar to mark it down on was a mystery known only to Chester. And perhaps the sow. Be that as it may, Dad would go out in the evening to take him his swill, and many times instead of a big black and white boar grunting over the trough there would be an empty pen and a gap in the fence where Chester had pried out the two bottom rails and squeezed through.

But Dad never worried about him. Everybody on Pleasant Ridge knew Chester. The farmer he visited would invite him into the pigpen to spend the night. Next morning, the breeding accomplished, he would turn him out and boost him toward home. A satisfied bass *oink* in his pen told us when he had returned. Dad went to feed him, and nearly every time he would find a used shotgun shell tied to Chester's corkscrew tail with a piece of binder twine. Stuffed inside the gunshell would be a tightly rolled dollar bill to pay the breeding fee. Our neighbors were honest, to be sure, and they appreciated an animal like Chester. Think how much time and trouble and how many trips to our place in a jolt wagon he must have saved them. Dad praised him to the skies, and this was natural, for it's true you won't find one boar hog in a thousand who can keep his own book and make his collections also. Dad could have forgiven Joseph if he had been any kind of an animal except a cat, or if he had been commercial like Chester and brought back folding money.

The same qualities that made Chester a darling of the neighborhood led Joseph to his downfall. Joseph took care of his own book, too—and I'm sure it was every bit as full as Chester's—and he covered the same number of barn lots. Farmers never invited him in to spend the night. They laid for him with brickbats and old shoes. And as for returning with a gunshell tied to his tail, the nearest Joseph ever came to that was to blow in home from a singing bee peppered with buckshot.

Strong family resemblances showed up now and then in the sackfuls of castaways the neighbors left in our driveway after dark. Here would be a kitten with a white triangle dabbed on one side of a spotted face; there a darkish fellow wearing a borrowed yellow tail; and over yonder a little fellow whose arrangement of spots was vaguely familiar. We slipped them into our collection without any awkward results.

But one April morning Dad came back to breakfast after his chores at the barn, and we heard him stop outside the door to the screened porch and say, "No! Oh, no. It can't be."

We never knew how they arrived without Hubert and me seeing them, but there were four honest-to-goodness little spitting images of Joseph rassling on the steps. Everything about them was complete, and almost identical: white vest, yellow tail, and spots like the mill ends of a calico factory. Dad couldn't mistake the source, for he saw Joseph in the easy chair just inside the screen. Sitting bowed over end-to-end, with one hind leg laid across his shoulder like a fishing pole, Joseph was busy tweezing a fresh deposit of buckshot out of the checkered fur piece he used for a seat.

"This is the end of that ornery tomcat," Dad shouted, stomping across the porch. "Ma can claim they're sent here for a sign if she wants to, but I'll be doggoned if I put up with a whole new generation of omens, four at a time. You boys don't need to put up a howl. That cat leaves this place, and there's no two ways about it."

Dad sat down to breakfast with his mouth drawn across his face in one straight line, which always meant the end of mere talk and the beginning of action. Hubert and I knew that the time for begging or arguing was past. Hubert asked him timidly how he meant to dispose of Joseph.

"Well, hanging's too good for him. I doubt if you could kill him with a shotgun. The neighbors have been trying it for some time. And he must be part fish, or he would have drowned in the rain the night he sneaked in

here. I'm going to Martinsburg Saturday to see about
trading mules with your Uncle John. I think I'll take the
rascal to your Aunt Emmy."

Mother said, "What if Sister Emmy doesn't happen
to want him?"

Dad said, "I won't ask her. I'll do her and John like
one of the neighbors just did me. An eye for an eye. An
old tomcat for four kittens. You know that thicket of
wild plums at the bend in the road just before you reach
John's barn? I'll stop behind it and put the cat in the
road. Then when he starts looking for something to eat,
Emmy will feed him and take him in. She's a cat fancier
like Ma and the boys." He turned to Hubert and me.
"You know he'll have a good home at your Aunt Emmy's,
and you boys can forget about him. One thing more.
After I haul that cat away from here we'll have no bellyaching about it. We won't mention him again. You boys
understand me?"

"Yes, sir. No bellyaching—on either side?"

"On either side."

Dad ignored Joseph the rest of the week. Joseph used
the easy chair; Dad politely sat on the lounge, biding his
time until Saturday. Friday night at the supper table, he
made Hubert and me a small peace offering: "Boys, I'll
tell you what we can do. I'll give you the money and you
can each buy a little Belgian hare from Truthful Thaddeus. Both males, of course. I don't want the place overrun with rabbits. But they're something nice to take care
of, and it will help you forget Joseph. What do you say?"

We turned his offer down flat. "We don't want to forget Joseph. We like cats. We don't like rabbits."

It surprised Dad, and angered him as well. He said, "Well, you'll *learn* to like 'em. Farm boys have to be interested in more important animals than cats."

Looking into her coffee cup, Grammaw said, "William, why don't you wait till you come back from Emmy's and see if you're still in the rabbit notion?"

"No, my mind's made up. They can get them in the morning before I start to Martinsburg. I'll go to Johnsons' and pick out two buck rabbits just to be sure. You couldn't trust a knucklehead like Thaddeus to tell the sex of a baby rabbit."

He brought back two silly, goggle-eyed little varmints with rat teeth and burro ears. He helped us knock together a pen of boards and chicken netting under the sweet-cherry trees. He was in a hurry to start to Martinsburg for it was a long, slow trip for the mare. Peter Rabbit turned his back and went to scrunching dry cherry pits. Cotton Bottom sat and twittered his nose. Dad reached down to pet him.

"Now that's the kind of an animal I like to see my boys —*ouch! dang you*—take an interest in," he said, and finished rather lamely as Cotton Bottom mistook his finger for a carrot. "I must find a box for that tomcat."

Joseph squirmed and kicked and made himself quite awkward for one person to cage, but Dad finally succeeded in holding him in a berry crate until he could nail the lid. The last we saw of Joseph as he rode down the driveway in the back of the buggy was a long, spotted front leg feeling through the slats of his prison for a latch.

Dad told Mother he would spend the night at Uncle John's and she need not look for him until Sunday afternoon. He was taking the back road to Martinsburg, eight miles away, by way of the community called Pull Tight. It was a rough, crooked trail of ruts and stones and tree roots, and Dad would not ask Old Nellie to make the return trip without a night's rest first.

Whistling "Oh Susannah," Hubert and I went to pick a basket of clover for Peter Rabbit and Cotton Bottom. We were more optimistic about Joseph's future than Dad suspected.

The story of us boys and the Belgian hares can be told in a few words. In less than a week they had dug out of their pen and run away. They were wild enough not to let themselves be caught, but tame enough to sneak to the truck patch for cabbage in the daytime and to clomp across the front porch at night hunting loose boards to stomp. Dad spent several weeks looking for their sleeping quarters. Finally he whistled for Dewey, our old black and white sheep dog, and set him on their trail. But they had located their hideout well enough to stump even a rabbit expert like Dewey.

One bright morning, a big buck rabbit came thumping out of the jimsonweeds by the hog-pen fence. It was Cotton Bottom, who was closely followed by a gaunt and proud-looking Peter Rabbit, who was closely followed by one-two-three-four-five-six little you-know-whats with rat teeth and burro ears. And almost before you could say Mr. McGregor there were three generations of Belgian hares in the truck patch helping Dad thin the cabbage.

Grammaw said, "Don't worry, William. You'll *learn* to like them."

The story of Joseph and Aunt Emmy can be told in still fewer words. When Dad returned from Martinsburg late Sunday afternoon he rued the day he had agreed to have no bellyaching about that ornery tomcat. The first thing he saw when he stepped on the screened porch was Joseph, flat on his back in the leather chair, fanning his bruised feet.

Joseph was still enjoying his hard-earned reprieve a few weeks later when strawberry season came around. The ripening berries lay fat and pink on the vines under a warm May sun. Dad said he would go for the pickers in a few days, and in the meantime he and Hubert and I would repair the crates and berry carriers.

The crating shed stood in a corner of the barn lot by the road, tucked under the edge of an ancient Early Harvest apple tree whose branches were valued more for the shade they cast than for the knotty fruit they bore. One side of the shed was hinged across the middle, so an upper portion of the board wall could be let down and supported to form a counter where berry pickers passed their full gallons inside to the crating bench. Dad opened this side of the shed and assembled his tools on the bench so he would be facing the soft breeze that riffled the tall grass under the apple tree.

Little Wilson tagged after us, and of course Joseph was there, winding around first one overall leg and then another. The two of them went outside to play, while Dad and Hubert and I worked. Wilson soon got tired, and he flopped down in the edge of the grass near some scraps of old lumber and half-rotten fenceposts stacked against the tree trunk. Joseph crawled into the curve of his arm; Wilson pulled his straw hat down over his eyes; they both lay there on their backs in the warm, sleepy shade.

Dad was fitting the handle into a berry carrier and Hubert and I were at the back of the shed, sorting through some broken boxes, when we heard Joseph utter a loud complaint.

"What's the matter out there?" Dad asked. "Having a bad dream?"

It was the low-pitched, undecided protest, half meow and half whine, that Joseph made in his throat when he saw a strange dog approaching. We heard it the second time.

Dad said, "Shut up. There's not a dog within half a mile of you."

He stood for a moment looking out the window.

"Wilson!" Dad said. He spoke softly, but the urgent way he clipped off the word startled us.

Hubert and I could not see under the apple tree from where we were, but we heard Wilson's drowsy answer: "Whaa . . . ?"

"Can you hear me all right?"

"Uh-huh."

"Listen to me carefully. I want you to play a little game with me. Just lie still while I'm talking to you. Remember how you boys sometimes play statue and don't move a muscle till the count is over? Well, if you can act like a statue till I count up to ten I'll give you a quarter. Five whole nickels. Think you can? No, don't get up. Just tell me if you want to play."

"I'll try it."

"Good. Now you're a statue. *One!* You mustn't say a word. You can't move even one finger or you lose your five nickels."

"What's the matter?" Hubert and I asked, puzzled.

Dad looked around. He held a finger to his lips. The *sh-h-h* he pronounced was more of a motion than a sound. Something in his manner and the chalk white tinge under his sunburn warned us that it was a serious game he was playing with Wilson.

"*Two!*" It was distinct, but not loud.

Joseph growled again. This time there was no uncertainty about it. Joseph was angry.

Still staring out the window, Dad let his hand slide along the bench where he had been nailing carriers. His fingers brushed the hammer, passed over it, and touched the hatchet. His hand closed around the handle and gripped it so hard his knuckles whitened.

"*Three!* I'm coming out there, Wilson. Don't pay any attention to me. Don't pay any attention to the cat, no matter what he does. Just be a good solid statue."

Dad stepped to the door, carefully pushed it open, stepped through, and carefully closed it behind him, evidently to keep the wind from slamming it. Hubert and I tiptoed to the window. We saw Wilson lying with his hat over his face. Joseph had crawled up from the curve of his arm, and he stood now with his front feet on Wilson's chest, looking over him into the scraps of bark and kindling on the other side. His tail was enlarged to a stiff brush, and he was threatening the pile of kindling with every one of his bared teeth.

"*Four!* You're doing fine, my boy. Keep quiet."

Dad came around in front of the window. Beads of sweat stood out on his upper lip.

I studied the pile of bark again to see if I could find what Joseph had found. Then it showed up like one of those loosely drawn picture puzzles in a magazine where you are supposed to find a hidden face. You turn the puzzle around this way and that, and it's nothing but twiggy branches and fluffy clouds, until all at once a face resolves out of the crooked lines, and you wonder why you hadn't noticed it before. Ever after that, the hidden face looms up like a calendar on the wall.

That's the way it was in the kindling scraps. As the eye rested on it, the second strip of bark from the edge was suddenly rounded on top and narrower than the others. What had appeared to be flecks of mold on a strip of rotten bark were evenly spaced markings on skin the color of dull metal. The eye followed it then, from a tapering tail over the short body and thick neck to the flat, three-cornered head and ugly veiled eyes a few inches from little Wilson's closed hand. Copperhead!

"*Five!* Here I come, Wilson. Keep still."

Dad was lifting his feet out of the tall grass, balancing himself and stepping again with the silence of a shadow.

I could feel the skin draw up on my flesh like cold wet chamois skin. A copperhead snake is the foulest creature a farmer knows. It doesn't warn you with a rattle. It doesn't give you notice by coiling up before it strikes. It lies motionless and hidden by its surroundings until it is disturbed; then it deals death with one quick blow. Wilson could have opened his pink and white fist and touched it.

"*Six!*"

Joseph pulled his hind feet up on Wilson's chest. His back rose in an arch, and he stood leaning backward as though braced against a strong wind. Hate and fear danced in his eyes like sparks struck from a flintstone.

"*Seven!*"

Dad was creeping closer. Joseph puffed up to his full, menacing height, the way he did when he was backed up in a corner by a dog four times his size. His head was pulled in between his shoulder blades; his mouth stretched open like a tiger rug. He shifted his weight on Wilson's chest. Wilson drew in a deep breath, for the cat was heavy.

"Careful! *Eight!* Don't move, Wilson."

Dad raised his hatchet above his head. The snake might have been lifeless, except for a slight adjustment of spots among the bark, and an almost unnoticeable thickening along its neck.

"*Nine!* Quiet, Wilson."

Joseph bunched his feet together and sprang into the bark with the same swift arc of motion he made when he nailed a mouse. The copperhead was quicker. The neck lashed up and straightened out, as an index finger does when released from the ball of the thumb in a hard thump. The flat three-cornered head struck Joseph's white vest front in midair.

With one movement of his front paw, Joseph swiped it to the ground, and an instant later he had sunk his long teeth in the back of its neck. The ugly reptile mouth gaped open; the head whipped back and forth in search of a place to bury its fangs the second time. Its whole struggling length whipped the ground in coiling and un-coiling loops of brown-spotted back and pale naked belly.

Dad threw Wilson out of the way and, stepping over the spot where he had lain, he brought his hatchet down and cut the snake in two. He placed his heavy shoe heel on the bloody stub of a head and pulled it away from Joseph. He cut it to pieces, and then in a frenzy of relief he went on chopping and chopping until not even a trace of the snake remained in the chips and pulverized ground. His shirt was dripping wet.

Joseph drew back and reached down and tried to lick away the sting of his wound. I picked him up to examine him. There was a lump the size of an acorn on his vest front. Two bloody pinpricks marked the skin on one side of the lump. Joseph tore himself out of my arms and climbed through the fence into the blackberry patch.

Little Wilson lay like a discarded statue in the grass where Dad had thrown him. Still playing the game, he had heard Dad say "Nine" and was patiently waiting for the final count. Later, at the house, he was puzzled because Mother and Grammaw hugged him so tightly and cried so hard. He knew that in some way he had become a hero, and he had five new nickels for his bank.

Grammaw went with Hubert and me to look for Joseph. We hunted up and down every row of the blackberry patch. We found him where he had crawled into the farthest corner, led by the instinct that compels a suffering cat to withdraw from all other animals. The ground under him had been kicked bare like a hen wallow, and there were swatches of many-colored fur on the briars where he had writhed in agony. He lay flat on his back, with all four feet pressed against his white vest. His body was stiffening, but still warm.

We put Joseph away nicely. We padded his coffin with an old quilt and lined it with pieces of lace curtain. It was a good strong coffin, made out of a wooden box. We thought Joseph deserved something more substantial than one of the pasteboard cartons we ordinarily buried our pets in. Hubert and I had been searching around in the wagon-shed loft among the empty boxes Dad stored there. We found one of the right size to hold Joseph's big heavy body. Hubert asked Dad if we might use it.

"Sure," he said. "Go ahead and take whichever one you want."

We dug the grave in our pet cemetery under a plum

tree beyond the pink chicken house. We were ready to
lower the coffin in the ground before we noticed the red
stencil on the end telling what the box had contained in
the first place. And thinking back over Joseph's eventful
life as we sadly shoveled the dirt into his grave, we
thought it seemed perfectly fitting that he should have
been laid to his eternal rest in a dynamite box.

Hubert was rounding up the grave while I carved
Joseph's name on the brick headstone, and Wilson carried flowers from the yard. After a while, Wilson came
back from the other side of the house with a big light-
green bouquet.

Hubert twisted the plants into a wreath, which he
laid against the headstone.

Wilson asked, "What is that stuff?"

"Here, smell it," Hubert said, rubbing a spicy leaf
between his fingers. "It's catnip. Where did you get it?"

"Daddy gave it to me. He said it was a farewell gift
for Joseph."

7

Reed-Organ Cowboy

GRAMMAW HAD BEEN LIVING WITH US A WHOLE YEAR BE-
fore becoming convinced that Hubert and I were deter-
mined to remain, and act like, boys until that longed-for
time when we would grow up and be men. It had been
a year when we were under the influence of Zane Grey
and intent on becoming cowboys. Grammaw had found
some of our wild west games a great handicap to neat
housekeeping and even, at times, a threat to the furniture itself. So she decided at this point to inject a little
culture into life on the range by having one of us take
organ lessons.

Being the older, I was the first and, as it turned out,
the only victim. She may have been planning to corral
Hubert in the same way a year or two later but, if so,
she abandoned the plan. In view of my experience at
the organ I think I know why. Due to Grammaw's per-
sistence and other circumstances beyond my control, I
soon achieved an outstanding notoriety as a keyboard
artist, and by the time I reached the age of fourteen
every farmer in the neighborhood looked upon me as a
freak of nature in the same class as a six-legged calf or an

apple tree that bore persimmons. I was the only boy on Pleasant Ridge who played a musical instrument.

At the time of Grammaw's momentous decision, we had a small flat-topped cherry-wood organ sitting idle in the parlor under its crocheted lambrequin and vases of dried honesty plant. Mother liked to play church music on its faded yellow keys, but with four children and all the work a farmer's wife had to do, she lacked the time. Mother had once suggested giving Devore lessons, but after waiting on Mother when Wilson was born (and being highly praised for it), Devore had decided that she wanted to be a nurse, and attending to the needs of her current doll took so much time that she would not be able to practice. And she got by with it. At least, temporarily.

Grammaw's inspiration came one morning while she was in the parlor, dusting the organ. She went straight to Mother with it. "Music hath charms," Grammaw quoted. She went on to say that Bruce might never learn to soothe the savage, but it would certainly mean less hollerin' and popgun shootin' and lassoin' around the house while he was in the parlor on the organ stool. Mother agreed with Grammaw that the organ might as well be put to some use, other than providing a nesting place for the mice.

Mother was further receptive to the idea because it so happened that one of her ambitions for her eldest son had begun to wither on the vine that same spring. Mother had always halfway hoped that I would turn out to be a Methodist minister. Perhaps she had been influenced by

my large vocabulary and forceful delivery of Sunday
school words and thought they could be channeled into
a more constructive use. At any rate, she had put me to
studying the Bible as soon as I'd learned to read.

My method of getting through the difficult passages
of the Old Testament was to attack them with all possible speed, the way a neighbor of ours rammed his
Overland touring car into a stretch of mud holes in the
road, hoping to clear the heavy passages by momentum.
Every so often I got stuck and had to back up and take
another run and a shoot into Genesis. That spring found
me bogged down as usual in the middle of Leviticus.
Mother said that a boy who had finished the seventh
grade without being able to read the Pentateuch probably wasn't cut out for the pulpit after all. She was pondering over the question of my future when Grammaw
suggested music.

And, by coincidence, Grammaw's bright idea occurred at a crucial point in my own plans. Not long
before that I'd been dismayed to overhear Dad telling
Mother that Bruce and Hubert were getting big enough
to take a more active interest in farm work, and with
this in mind he had decided to set out four acres of
Aroma strawberries instead of our usual single acre.

Nearly every farmer in the Knobs grew strawberries
and shipped them to the Chicago market. Like all the
other men in the neighborhood, Dad took his sons with
him to the berry patch and put them to pulling weeds.
Like all the other boys on Pleasant Ridge, Hubert and
I had long since agreed that we would rather run from

weeds any day than fight them. And four acres of strawberries meant *twenty-four thousand* healthy plants to
grow and multiply and be crawled over and hand-weeded,
row by row! It would have played havoc with any boy's
plans for the summer. And thus I felt that fate had intervened in my behalf.

It was hard to picture any of my cowpoke heroes in
chaps and spurs taking music lessons, pumping and
thumping away at our cherry-wood organ. But at least
up to the end of *The U. P. Trail*, not one of them had
ever faced four acres of weeds waiting to be pulled. I
was at my wit's end. I made a pretense of balking at the
lessons until Grammaw offered to buy me a Brownie
box camera, and then said I was willing to take for a
while. Grammaw said to Mother, "Better telephone Miss
Jenkins while the brandin' iron is hot."

Miss Jenkins was a tall, raw-boned woman who lived
in Borden and drove a music route in the country several days of the week, similar to the Rawleigh Man, who
came around periodically in his black wagon peddling
extracts and household remedies. She made her rounds
in a clattering buggy, drawn by a long-legged sorrel mare
named Maudie. In their faces, Miss Jenkins and Maudie
bore a certain resemblance. Each had a straight black
forelock, large brown eyes, and long angular features.
Miss Jenkins's bony face wore a hard-pressed look, as
though she might be running late for her next music
lesson, while Maudie seemed not to give a darn whether
they made it that same day or not. Miss Jenkins tried
to hurry her from one house to the next. She whacked

the lines across the tall slope of the mare's rump and
urged in a sing-song, "Get up, Maudie . . . (*whack*)
. . . Get up, Maudie . . . (*whack*)," the same as she
tapped her pencil on the organ and chanted, "One-and-
two-and." Maudie always traveled at her same indifferent
trot, regardless, and so Miss Jenkins's prompting had
more the effect of keeping her in rhythm than it did of
increasing her speed. They covered Pleasant Ridge on
Thursdays.

Miss Jenkins told Mother she would be delighted to
try to teach me. Of course, she had never had a boy
pupil before, and this would be an opportunity to break
new ground, so to speak. The next Thursday afternoon
at three o'clock, she and Maudie came clattering up our
driveway to turn the first shovelful. Miss Jenkins wore
a long, high-waisted black skirt, a crumpled, second-best
white silk blouse, wet under the arms, and a frayed band
of red velvet pinned around her neck with a cameo. The
April day was warm, and I noticed that she brought a
faint trace of Maudie's presence into the parlor with her.
A pair of eyeglasses hung on a reel at her shoulder. She
zipped the chain out of the reel, pinched the glasses on
her nose, and my musical career began.

Miss Jenkins opened Langdon's *Reed Organ Method*
to page one and showed me the long black lines in sets
of five, sprinkled with black and white characters called
notes. It was simple enough to remember that the loca-
tion of a note among the lines and spaces told you which
key to press on the organ; and the stems and flags, how
many to count while you held it down. I had to remem-

ber to keep the organ pedalled full of air but, outside of that, learning music promised to be as easy as falling off a log, certainly much easier than pulling weeds or reading the Pentateuch.

After the lesson, Mother came in to pay Miss Jenkins her thirty-five cents. Miss Jenkins's long bony face broke into a smile and her nostrils flared until for a moment I thought she was going to whinny. "Ooh!" she said. "Bruce takes to the organ just like a duck to water."

I took to the organ exactly four days the following week, this being the length of time it took Dad, with Hubert's help, to weed and hoe the strawberries. Alerted right after breakfast each morning by the sound of Dad's hoe being filed in the toolshed, I took to the organ and began a C scale, loud, slow, and clear. Between my carefully spaced do-re-mi's I heard Dad calling for us boys, and Mother telling him to take Hubert and go ahead, she'd send Bruce as soon as he finished practicing. I managed to drag it out and stroll to the berry patch and show my willingness to work just as Dad was hanging his hoe on the fence to go to dinner. Sitting on an organ stool for the better part of four days, you can't help learning some music, even when you hold *Riders of the Purple Sage* in one hand and sound only enough notes per hour with the other to avoid suspicion among your listeners. By the next Thursday afternoon I had gone two measures beyond my assignment in the book. Miss Jenkins all but kicked up her heels in sheer delight.

Of all the many labor-saving devices that I had tried, the organ proved to be the most versatile. One of the built-in advantages was a tendency of its keys to stick in rainy weather. The effect of four or five keys stuck down and blaring through my melodic little waltzes was so disagreeable as far away as the kitchen that I was quickly excused to go and play. If in Dad's judgment the ground was too wet to work and still not enough keys were sticking to attract attention, I used an invention of my own. I pumped the organ up to full volume and stood Joseph on one end of the keyboard and another kitten of equal size on the opposite end. Between the growl coming out of the bass and the shrill discord sounding in the treble I began plowing out "The Happy Farmer" in the middle of the keyboard. Either Mother or Grammaw, whichever one was closer, came running to yell outside the parlor door that I had better wait until the organ dried out.

Also, it eliminated much of the drudgery of daily chores. During the times when the strawberries happened not to need weeding, I readjusted my practicing schedule. Instead of applying myself for long tiresome periods at a time, I learned that I could accomplish more in short, carefully spaced odd moments. So I stood ready to run to the parlor and sound off at the drop of a hat or, more accurately speaking, at the rattle of a dipper in the empty water bucket. Mother hated to tear me away in the middle of a piece; so Hubert carried most of the drinking water from the spring. It was seldom that Grammaw's call for cookstove wood caught me too unaware to hightail it to the parlor; so Hubert carried most of the cookstove wood. Late in the afternoon, Mother would decide that it was time for us to shell corn for the chickens. She would corner Hubert and start him toward the barn, wondering where I had disappeared. "Orvetta Waltz" came pumping out of the parlor, and she knew; so Hubert shelled most of the corn. "Heck of a cowboy you are," he often said to me. "Why don't you take off your chaps and put on a petticoat? You won't ever catch me playin' on that old organ." Hubert failed to realize which side of a fellow's bread was buttered.

Weed pulling and other chores kept Hubert busy outdoors and confined me to the parlor the biggest part of that summer. By the time school began in the fall I was able to play the first four measures of "Jenny Lind's Favorite Polka" on page fifty-two, and Miss Jenkins had spoken of starting me on sheet music. One afternoon she and Mother and Grammaw sat visiting over the hot chocolate that usually followed the lesson, and Miss Jenkins asked if Mother planned to have me take during the winter. Mother said she guessed not. She explained that we could never build a fire in the parlor fireplace because of the swallows that nested in the chimney, and the room was always closed up when the weather turned cold.

"What a pity!" Miss Jenkins sighed, slapping at a fly that hovered over her chocolate. "Right when Bruce is doing *so* well!" And how she wished that her girl pupils were half as devoted to their music.

Mother said, "Yes, it seems too bad, but it can't be helped."

Grammaw said, "I wonder . . ."

A few mornings later I was happy to look out a window and see the vegetation lying crisp under a heavy blanket of frost. It meant the end of the weed-pulling, for sure. Cold weather would soon follow and end the practicing. I put on a long face equal to Miss Jenkins's woebegone countenance and, to make it convincing, I strongly expressed my opinion of the chimney swallows who were responsible for the untimely end of my musical career.

I came home from school one sunny afternoon when there was a nip of coming frost in the air and it was actually warmer outdoors than in an unheated room. I knew there was no danger of being sent to the parlor, and so I was ready to get my jumping rope and help Hubert lasso the suckling calves in the barn. A small hickory log blazed in the fireplace of the dining room. The door was propped open into the sitting room. Looking in, under the impression that we had visitors, I saw the organ sitting up against the front wall, with the book on the music rack opened to page fifty-two.

Mother said, "Hand me your lunch pail and go and start your practicing. Since you felt so strongly about it, Grammaw and I decided that it wouldn't be fair to deprive you of your music on account of what you called 'those confounded old birds.' Miss Jenkins has changed your lesson day to Saturday."

For a solid hour every afternoon that winter, and a half day on Saturday, while Hubert and Truthful Thaddeus trapped rabbits and went coasting and snowball fighting, I sat on the cool organ stool and played "Jenny Lind's Favorite Polka." The way I performed it under the circumstances, I'm sure that Jenny, too, would have renounced it long before spring.

The next summer started out much the same: another big strawberry patch, more music lessons. The Good Lord saw fit to send an abundance of weeds and, of equal importance, to preserve Hubert's stupidity. This kept him humping over the berry rows one hot day after another and fixed me to the keyboard with a dedication that by the middle of August had taken me through the instruction book, "Falling Waters," and the "Edelweiss Glide Waltz."

For some time I had been casting about for a fool-proof way to keep the organ out of the sitting room the second winter, facing somewhat the same problem as the poor fellow who was trying so desperately to find the Lost Chord. As the words of the song put it:

> Seated one day [Thursday morning] at the organ,
> I was weary and ill at ease;
> And my fingers wandered idly
> Over the noisy keys.
> I know not what I was playing,
> Nor what I was thinking then;
> But I struck one chord of music—

—and I noticed something radically wrong with the chord of music I struck. Middle C failed to omit its usual clear singing tone and, no matter how much pressure I applied to the pedals, merely blew out a stream of air like a tired sigh instead.

Mother said, "I wonder what happened. Maybe a mouse has been gnawing on the reed."

Grammaw said, "Guess again. The mice all moved out of the organ the day Two-Gun Butch had his first lesson."

Miss Jenkins turned out to be an organ mechanic as well a music teacher. That afternoon, she unscrewed the back of the organ, got down on her haunches with a queer-looking device called a reed hook, and extracted the ailing middle C and its whole long stick of accoutrements. She tapped the apparatus on the floor and finally dislodged a toothpick that in some mysterious way had worked down through the keyboard. Middle C responded with its usual clear singing tone and at the same time pointed to the Grand Amen of organ practice that I had been seeking.

The organ was old—Mother told Miss Jenkins that she had bought it second-hand when she started keeping house—and it had served its time. It was possible that by cold weather its playing condition might not warrant dragging it across the hall. So I made sure it wasn't long until most of the white keys and a few of the black ones began to sigh or wheeze or whistle or remain dead silent when pressed down. Miss Jenkins spent a good part of each lesson period on her haunches, extracting reeds and covering the parlor carpet with matches, buttons, hairpins, bread crumbs, feathers, and leaves of dried honesty plant that in some mysterious way had worked down through the keyboard. She fought a losing battle, though, for she had only thirty minutes a week at our house and I had seven whole days.

Luck was with me. Frost laid the weeds low one night in September. Within a week the organ had shot its wad. School began the following Monday. I didn't feel completely safe until there was no possibility of repairing the organ. Mother took the cherry-wood cabinet and made a chest for bedclothes. I waited for Dad to dispose of the remains. He had a habit of gathering up every worn-out object around the place and storing it for some possible use in the future. Naturally, according to his theory, there was sure to come a time in every farmer's life when nothing would fill his particular need like the insides of an old broken-down reed organ, and so he stored it in the wagonshed loft with all the other forgotten junk. It was as good as buried, and my winter was secure.

After the first day of school I hurried home to saddle up one of the old work horses and gallop off into the sunset over our back cow pasture, and I found Mother and Grammaw seated in the dining room busy with their crochet hooks.

Mother said, "Go and look in the parlor."

Grammaw smiled over the doily she was crocheting.

Even the strong odor of varnished oak permeating the hall failed to prepare me for what I saw. Mother had sent for and gotten the biggest and fanciest Beckwith organ that Sears Roebuck manufactured. All the neighbors agreed later that it was by far the finest piece of furniture ever to be delivered on Pleasant Ridge. Between the red-carpeted pedals and the wide horizontal band of jigsaw scallops that barely cleared the ceiling there was the large playing cabinet of quarter-sawed golden oak with a six-octave keyboard, and above that another oaken structure with a large square mirror in the center, which was flanked on each side by scrollwork, small oblong mirrors set vertically, machine-turned wooden columns, red cloth inserts behind carved grill-work, a cabinet for sheet music, and a series of shelves in graduated sizes for doilies and the overflow from the whatnot.

The instrument was set in the alcove by the fireplace and angled so that its mirrors seemed to double the size of the parlor. It reflected the walls of rosebud-and-lattice paper, multiplied the hanging lamp and its cut-glass pendants by two, and exposed the porcelain rears of George and Martha Washington standing among the vases of peacock feathers and dried honesty plant on the mantel. There was no doubt about it, the neighbor women said enviously, the new organ simply *made* the parlor.

Not that it stayed there long. The temperature dropped into the thirties that night. Mother called Dad and Chod in to help, and until the next spring the new organ simply *made* the sitting room.

Miss Jenkins skipped around the Beckwith, admiring every detail. "Oooooh! Isn't it just perfect," she exclaimed. "Six octaves! Eleven stops! What volume! And such a splendid tone! Now Bruce can really go places with his music. When you've got a Beckwith you've got something. They just last for-*ever*! Oooooh!" Giving a great sigh of pleasure, she pinched her glasses on her nose and the long, hard winter set in.

With an indestructible new instrument under my fists and the constant encouragement and supervision of Mother and Grammaw and Miss Jenkins and a heavy stand of weeds three years in a row, there was no way to go in my music except forward—which I did with breathtaking speed.

Miss Jenkins now boasted of me as her star pupil. Many of the neighbors in whose homes I performed called me the Boy Wonder of Pleasant Ridge. Hubert and the boys at school called me by other names. My reputation spread through the Knobs like a brushfire before the wind. The crowning acknowledgment of my talent was an invitation to play in stuck-up Chapel Knob Church, five miles to the south of us.

Chapel Knob was a well-to-do community, and the church was the largest and most elegant we had ever seen. Panes of bright-colored glass outlined the windows, separate Sunday school rooms opened off from the main auditorium through sliding doors, a baptizing tank lay under the removable floor in back of the pulpit, and the only carbide lights in the Knobs (excepting those at the McKinley Hotel) hung from the ceiling in polished metal shades.

The members of the congregation were noted for their piety as well as their prosperity. They didn't believe in dancing, card playing, ice cream suppers, or admitting anybody into Heaven who had not donated substantially to Chapel Knob Church. They looked down their noses at outsiders, and they made it a rule to go to church every time the doors were opened. If the Brown family didn't feel like attending morning worship some Sunday, they got ready and went anyhow because they were afraid to stay away. Not that God wouldn't have overlooked their absence if there had been a good reason for it, but the Smith family would be there to count noses and start an ugly rumor. The Smiths' criticism, or the Browns' in their turn, was a lot more to be feared than God's, because for one thing it spread so much faster, and so the preacher always faced the entire congregation.

The biggest toad in the Chapel Knob puddle was Deacon Bradford, a man with thin sandy hair, a neat sandy mustache, brilliant teeth, and a smooth, wheedling manner that suited his occupation, which was dealing in livestock. The people bowed down to Deacon Bradford on Sunday, but there was hardly a man in the congregation who would have risked trading horses with him through the week. He had a daughter, Cecelia, who took lessons in Town. He was always putting her up to play in public. She was said to be a great show-off, although I had never heard her play.

One spring morning Deacon Bradford telephoned Mother and asked if she would let me play an organ solo at their Children's Day exercises, which was something like a Last Day of School, with music and a religious theme. Mother declined. She said it was so far away, and Bruce had never played in a church, and she was afraid his music wouldn't please the congregation. One reason, which Mother didn't mention, was that she disliked going to Chapel Knob. We were used to the

community church on Pleasant Ridge, where visitors
were made especially welcome, not given the cold shoulder. We had been to Chapel Knob during revivals or at
funerals, but Mother always said the atmosphere made
her uncomfortable. Grammaw said, "Yes. You feel like
you're trespassin' in the anteroom of Heaven."

Deacon Bradford began to coax. "Now, now, Mrs.
Bell," he said, and Mother said afterward that he seemed
to be patting her shoulder over the telephone. "You're
too modest about that boy of yours. You mustn't hide
his light under a bushel, you know. And as for the organ
solo, Mrs. Bell, it won't necessarily have to be a sacred
number. Innocent little hands at the keyboard have a
way of glorifying any kind of music, don't you agree?"

Mother said, "I'll have to admit I hadn't looked at it
from that angle." The deacon insisted, and Mother promised to think it over and call him back.

As for me, getting my hands on the organ at Chapel
Knob had long been one of my secret ambitions. It was
fully as large from front to back as the bran box in our
cow stable, with a fine tone and plenty of power to fill
the auditorium. The church organist, Mrs. Blackman,
was an elderly woman in frail health and I knew she
wasn't getting out of the instrument a half of what was
really in it. It had twenty-one stops, but Mrs. Blackman
rarely used more than eight. I'd always wondered what
it would sound like wide open, with a younger pair of
legs working the pedals. I persuaded Mother to ask Miss
Jenkins what she thought about the Children's Day exercises.

"Oooooh! Chapel Knob!" exclaimed Miss Jenkins. "Aren't you just tickled pink? Of course Bruce will play."

She brushed Mother and all of her objections to one side and sped to the phone to tell Deacon Bradford how flattered we were at the invitation. This was early in April, and the program was to be given the latter part of May. Miss Jenkins sat right down and started thumbing through her sheet-music catalogs for the number that would show off her star pupil to best advantage.

My own choice would have been "Napoleon's Last Charge," by E. T. Paull. It was one of a number of "descriptive marches," as they were called, which Mr. Paull had composed to represent various exciting events in history, from "The Burning of Rome" to "Paul Revere's Ride." Printed captions above the music like "Flames Raging Fiercely" and "Populace Alarmed" advised the player as he went along, though not always the audience, what the noise was all about. Miss Jenkins taught them to her advanced pupils. I played a music roll full of them at every neighborhood party I attended, unless something happened to discourage me, such as all the guests getting up and going home.

"Napoleon's Last Charge" was a loud battle-whanging number, written in lurching 6/8 time and full of bugle calls and bloodshed. It built up to a climax on page seven. This part, labeled "Death in the Sunken Trenches," stiffened my audiences and raised them a couple of inches out of their chairs when I turned the page and galloped headlong into that mass of black notes, and they never

eased down completely (if they were still in the room)
until I had slain the last foot soldier and bugled the
victors off the field at the bottom of page ten. Grammaw
always said after hearing "Napoleon's Last Charge" on
the Beckwith that it was hard to understand how one
small boy could kick up so much music out of an innocent piece of furniture. She said Cowboy Joe knew what
his real calling was, after all. She asked Mother, "Why
don't you write to Sears Roebuck and see if they have a
saddle that will fit the organ stool?"

I thought the combination of "Napoleon's Last Charge"
and my innocent little hands on the twenty-one-stop
organ at Chapel Knob would, to quote Deacon Bradford, glorify the Children's Day program about right.
But Miss Jenkins put her foot down. "No, indeed," she
said. "Remember, the congregation there is very, *very*
devout, and if you play anything but a sacred number
they'll never stop gossiping." She told me that my selection would be "In the Sweet Bye and Bye with Variations" by Drumheller.

It was the kind of music that Miss Jenkins favored—
an old familiar tune disguised with "Variations." The
melody was repeated over and over, but concealed each
time within a different pattern of rippling runs, chitter-
ing chords, or tiddling octaves:

> In the Swee-EE-EE-EET (tiddle-tiddle-de-tweet)
> Bye and Bye—II-II-II (diddle-diddle-de-die).

Miss Jenkins took away my other pieces and set me to

memorizing the eight pages of Drumheller's "Variations."
This was contrary to the way she usually taught. Miss
Jenkins forbade her pupils to learn music by heart, as
she said it interfered with their sight-reading. In my
whole repertoire I had but one piece I could play without the notes—a song I had ordered from the music catalog and learned in secret. I thought it best not to let anyone know that I owned it, because I had borrowed the
thirty cents from the sugar bowl. I had memorized it by
constant repetition—when the house was empty.

Miss Jenkins considered Chapel Knob important
enough to make an exception and leave my music roll
at home. For a small boy to sit down at that big organ
and toss off eight pages of "Variations" without a note
to look at—well, it would certainly advertise his teacher.
She made one more suggestion: as long as I was going to
play a solo and would not be needed at rehearsals, I
should stay away from Chapel Knob until the night of
the program. Then everyone in the house would share
the thrill of hearing the Boy Wonder of Pleasant Ridge
for the first time. "Just like a bomb bursting in air,"
she told Mother, little knowing whereof she spoke.

Memorizing the "Variations" took less than two weeks,
leaving a month to ripple the runs, chitter the chords,
tiddle the octaves, and dwell on the rests in the left hand.
There was a good reason for paying careful attention to
these rests and giving them perhaps a shade more than
their actual time value. A few weeks earlier I had sent
in the correct solution to a puzzle in a farm paper and
received a gold ring as first prize. It was a loose fit on the

middle finger of my left hand and set with a flashing red stone the size of a nickel that for a long time I believed to be a "genu-wine" ruby. I took pains to bring out the left-hand rests prominently whenever I played in public, for fear that somebody in the audience, especially if seated in a far corner of the room, might not be given an opportunity to admire the ruby. The discreet little rests that Miss Jenkins taught me, with fingers dangling at eyebrow level, would be lost in the huge auditorium at Chapel Knob. So, keeping in mind the people who would be sitting in rear pews, I perfected the rests of "In the Sweet Bye and Bye" until they reached the altitude of distant farewell gestures made from a receding ocean liner.

The nearer the night of the program came, the more anxiously the family watched the calendar. Seven days, six days, now only five. Soon it would be over, and never again, they hoped, would

> In the Swee-EE-EE-EET (tiddle-tiddle-de-tweet)
> Bye and Bye-II-II-II (diddle-diddle-de-die)

come throbbing out of the parlor on the hot summer air. I, too, was counting the days until the last Sunday in May, when my artistry would be fully appreciated.

Chapel Knob Church was packed to the vestibule that night, and the doors to the Sunday school section had been scooted open to take care of the overflow. Vases of lilacs and dogwood bloom and woods ferns gave the platform a holiday look. Purple and gold crepe-paper bows fluttered over the windows, and mottoes such as "We Are Willing Little Helpers" were tacked up on the wall in twelve-inch cardboard letters to carry out the spirit of Children's Day.

Miss Jenkins had arrived early in order to allow Maudie a good rest before the nine-mile drive back to Borden. Wearing a flowered pink dress and a broad pink hat with black upright plumes like those on a hearse, she was sitting and fidgeting in the Amen corner. (Miss Jenkins, that is. Maudie was leaning against a hitching post by the graveyard, fast asleep.) Mother and Dad and Grammaw were given seats near the rear of the house, and Deacon Bradford ushered me into a reserved section with the other young people who were taking part. He handed me a sheet of paper with only the order of our performances written on it. The buzzing of the congregation died down. Deacon Bradford rose to make his opening remarks and announce the first number.

A quick look at the program showed that he had listed me as "Organ Solo" on the tail end of the evening. Just before my number there was a "Song and Pantomime" by the Intermediate Girls and, ahead of that, another "Organ Solo," this one by Deacon Bradford's daughter, Cecelia.

Cecelia was about sixteen years old, wide-toothed, red-faced, and by far the fattest girl I had ever seen. Seated on the organ stool, she hung down over it in folds, reminding me of Grammaw's salt-rising dough overflowing a crock. She accompanied several songs and musical recitations, and was immensely pleased with her own playing.

Her round, harvest moon face shone in a brighter shade of red, and her nose stuck up farther in the air each time she rolled off the organ stool and swaggered heavily to her pew. I felt that she was putting on rather elaborate airs for an organist who thus far had used no more than ten stops out of the available twenty-one, and when at last it came time for her solo I was frankly disgusted at the unnecessary ceremony she made of a simple thing like preparing the organ. She sat down and carefully tested the knee swells to see if they had been damaged since she'd accompanied the Young People's Choir in "Onward, Christian Soldiers." She drew out a handful of stops, scowled at the names, pushed them back, and after much pondering and changing selected the twelve she wanted. All right for you, Miss Fatty, I thought, as she took out a large white handkerchief and began to wipe her sweaty fingers. Show off all you like. You won't feel so proud after I perform. Cecelia laid her handkerchief on the organ top and sounded three slow chords. My spirits tumbled right down to the soles of my new patent leather button shoes.

In the Swee-EE-EE-EET (tiddle-tiddle-de-tweet)
Bye and Bye-II-II-II (diddle-diddle-de-die)

My number! Same tune, same variations. And the same rests! I looked desperately at Miss Jenkins in the Amen corner. Her long bony face was sagging under the pink hat. In planning to spring me as a big surprise it had never entered her mind that another soloist might choose the identical number. Certainly she knew that I couldn't follow Cecelia to the organ and repeat eight pages of tiddle-de-tweet. But as to what I could do instead, Miss Jenkins had no idea. Poor Miss Jenkins, sitting there with a notebook in her purse, ready to accept a shower of congratulations and new pupils the first thing after the benediction. Her black plumes resembled the decorations on a hearse, sure enough.

Cecelia chittered through her solo to the final chord. She closed the stops and waddled to her seat, looking strained and proud like a crimson-faced goose after laying an outsize egg. Sighs and whispers of admiration rustled through the congregation. Deacon Bradford sat smiling at his fingernails as though he had just got the better of somebody in a horse trade. Little Mrs. Blackman took her place at the organ to play for the pantomime.

It was "Jesus Wants Me for a Sunbeam," sung and acted out by sixteen of the Intermediate Girls, dressed in white cheesecloth robes with gold tinsel wrapped around their foreheads to represent sunbeams. They lined up on the platform and began to sing.

I turned around and looked at the family. Grammaw was studying one of the carbide lights overhead. Dad was just sitting there. Mother looked at me and shook her head. That could have meant one of several things: "I tried to talk you out of it in the first place." Or, "Just don't play." Or, "I don't know, either, what to do about it."

In a few minutes now, Deacon Bradford was going to

announce my solo. The question was, would I sit there
like a bump on a log and pretend to be absent? No, I
could not, because I was a stranger in the congregation,
and everybody in the house would be staring at me. . . .
Maybe I could stand up and say politely, "Ladies and
gentlemen, you'll have to excuse me. I'm sick to my
stomach." But the program would fizzle out without the
final number and, besides, I'd miss the chance of a life-
time at that powerful organ. . . . Not me! I'd go up
there and play something. . . . But what? . . . Perhaps
I could take the Chapel Knob hymn book and play my
favorite song with a few extra flourishes. . . . Song!
The word clicked. . . . There was the song I had memorized and played in secret. It was foolish of me not to
have thought of that at once. It was not a sacred number
as Miss Jenkins preferred, but Deacon Bradford had said
innocent little hands at the keyboard glorified any kind
of music. I went over the song swiftly in my mind to be
sure I remembered it. In some measures every other
count in the left hand was a rest—where they were needed
to display the ruby. In a second's time I had decided to
play it in double-quick tempo and with such fire and
abandon that Chapel Knob would never know but what
it was the selection that Miss Jenkins had drilled me on
since the first of April. Another second went by, and I
had also decided to teach Cecelia Bradford a few things
about showmanship. I breathed a sigh of relief—and self-
admiration. Not many boys of my age could have leaped
into a breach as I was about to do. And as the girls began
the last verse of "Jesus Wants Me for a Sunbeam," I was

crouched on the edge of the pew ready to make the leap.
They finished the last chorus. Sixteen dainty cheesecloth and tinsel sunbeams tiptoed from the platform and
faded into the vestry. A hush lingered over the audience.
Deacon Bradford stood up.

"Our concluding number will be an organ solo by a
young visitor from Pleasant Ridge." He paused and
smiled, briefly baring the edge of his teeth. "Now this
lad's mother tried to persuade me that he was not prepared to play in a church like Chapel Knob, and she said
perhaps his music might not find favor with our congregation. However, I insisted, and I know you will thank
me for the lovely solo you are about to hear. Master
Bruce Bell!"

I strode down the aisle to the organ, where I turned
and faced the house. With both arms straight out at the
sides and palms up, I swept the congregation a graceful
bow, somewhat in the shape of a horseshoe, and in fact
so far down I all but tumbled into the thick red carpet.
Next, I tested the organ stool for the proper elevation.
I twisted it up a half turn, seated myself, frowned, got
up, and twisted it down a quarter turn. After doing this
five or six times, maybe seven, I sat down once more, and
to show that I had at last hit upon the fine shade of adjustment I wanted, I let a tiny smile of relief play over
my features, like a person having a spot scratched that
has been itching him a long time. Then at the risk of
making myself conspicuous, I held my hand up in the
strong light and turned the ring around on my finger
and shook it several times to make sure the ruby had not

come loose in the setting. It seemed to be holding well enough, and so I examined the organ stops. Cecelia Bradford had made such a scene, pretending that she couldn't decide on the combination she wished to use. But I was one organist who knew beforehand exactly how he wanted his music to sound. Hesitating only long enough to read and approve their names, I began at the end and, going left to right, pulled out all twenty-one stops. I waited a few seconds—to create the proper suspense—then I pushed the knee swells open to their utmost volume, pumped the organ up to the bursting point and, after observing a long left-hand rest that pointed skyward like a steeple, I bent over the keyboard and tore into "Alexander's Ragtime Band."

This concluded the program. There is a possibility that it might have done so even if not scheduled by Deacon Bradford as the finale. Mother and Dad escorted me from the church, each grasping a wrist, and at the longest steps I had seen in use since watching Truthful Thaddeus flee from an enraged bull. Every face in the congregation had a little skift of ice on it, and Deacon Bradford's was frozen clear over. Miss Jenkins joined us outside, and while Dad was gone for the team and surrey she and Mother found a lot to say about my organ playing. Speaking simultaneously, and fast, they were hard to understand, and if a word was said in my favor I missed it. Dad drove up and we prepared to leave.

Grammaw ignored the frigid stares all about her and came skimming down the walk in her long black skirt, stiff as a ramrod under her little skillet-shaped black hat, with its crepe veil flowing out in back. As she started to enter the surrey she laid her hand on my shoulder for support. Her soft bony fingers tightened for an instant. Just before she placed her foot on the step and mounted in great dignity to the surrey seat, she leaned over and said softly but distinctly in my ear: *"Ride 'em, cowboy."*

8
Putting On Style

ONE OF THE ENJOYABLE FEATURES ABOUT LIFE ON A BIG
farm, as Grammaw had discovered shortly after coming
to Pleasant Ridge, was that it gave her an unlimited opportunity to entertain visitors, especially those who favored country cooking. Grammaw, the same as Mother
and Dad, loved people, and there was seldom a time
when they weren't "fixing for company," as Grammaw
put it. And by observing the room they reddened up,
Hubert and I could come pretty close to guessing who
was expected.

If Grammaw changed the checkered tablecloth in the
dining room between meals and scrubbed the brick
hearth to a brighter shade of red than usual, we looked
for a neighbor woman to come calling. Or, again, it
might mean that this was the day for the pack peddler
or the Rawleigh Man to stop. People who were used to
our ways were entertained in the room we lived in most
of the time, where the furniture was shabby and friendly.

The sitting room with its folding bed and marble-
topped tables served the purpose for preachers of most
denominations, our school teacher, and relatives on both
sides of the family. Grammaw whisked away the odds

and ends of clothing that had been tossed there, brushed the faded red carpet, and laid fresh tidies on the chairs. The bed in Mother's room between this and the dining room was spread with the silk coverlid in the Friendship pattern and used for hats and wraps.

But when Mother and Grammaw both put on dust-caps and pried up the parlor windows, that was a horse of another color. It meant that people were coming to stay all day Sunday, fine-haired visitors requiring our best behavior, Mother's gold-banded wedding dishes, and a dinner that began with chicken and dumplings and ended with steamed bag pudding. First, Mother and Grammaw carried great armloads of things from the parlor whatnot to the front porch to be aired and dusted. It took them all morning then to drag the heavy furniture back and forth, featherdust the gilt and curlicue picture frames, and polish the ornaments. When they ended up worn-out and dusty at dinnertime, the parlor was closed up like a sanctuary of plush and lace and china, and no one dared peek into it until Sunday morning, not even for my most urgent organ practice.

After the proper room had been made ready for the company, Grammaw took a bucket of hot soapsuds and went to freshen up the most important place of all, which was the little annex at the end of the garden path. No matter who the guests were, whether of parlor, sitting-room, or merely dining-room importance, they were equally apt to view this apartment at close range during their visit. Grammaw took extra pains there, because she believed that the state of cleanliness in the toilet revealed a woman's housekeeping habits more accurately than the more visible parts of the dwelling itself. Sooner or later, she measured every housewife on Pleasant Ridge by this same yardstick.

Grammaw scorned the usual practice of running a finger over a surface to test it for dust or, as some of the really snoopy women did, of opening a closet door with the pretense that she thought it led to another room. Grammaw politely excused herself and asked how to reach the backhouse. Her critical eyes examined it for muddy tracks on the floor, a litter of paper scraps, or portholes improperly capped with a piece of old rotten board. If she found these or other signs of neglect, she put the woman down as a housekeeper who cleaned only on the surface and who probably left carpet fuzz under the bed, or used her dishrag to wipe pot black off the cookstove. Grammaw took pride in keeping the toilet at our house above criticism, and when she first came to live with us she had been quite pleased to find such good material to work with.

It was painted inside and out in the same restful shade of dove-gray and surrounded on three sides by tall gooseberry bushes. It stood on two-by-fours sunk in concrete, solid and four-square to all the winds that blew and a challenge year after year to the Halloween pranksters who bruised their shoulders trying in vain to tip it. There were roomy accommodations for two full-size passengers, and a small, what you might call half-fare, seat in the corner. We boys, including Wilson, had abandoned this junior seat in favor of the grown-up bench as soon

as we could do so without too much overhang, and so it held the Sears catalog and the lime bucket and the tiny wooden shovel.

Grammaw never knew when visitors would drop in without warning. She spent so much time keeping the toilet in a presentable state that Dad and Chod and we boys would sometimes take to the bushes rather than wait till Grammaw finished sloshing around with her scrub brush. When she finally poured the rinse water in the zinnia bed along the path and came to the house, you knew she had left the place nice enough for Mrs. Vanderbilt or the stiffest Methodist preacher.

Grammaw loved those Sundays when she and Mother could clean and bake and cook up everything on the farm and put on style fit to kill. She loved to entertain people who were *somebody*, so she could elevate her little finger on her coffee cup and talk proper and be starched and polished and wear a strained, elegant look on her face all day. And she loved to make the whole family over, temporarily, for the benefit of the stylish company. The only drawback to all this was that when we had guests of the parlor caliber, she knew she could expect Hubert and me to flunk miserably in deportment.

Mother told Grammaw not to worry so much about us. "Boys will be boys, Ma," she said, "and you can't make girls or old men out of them." As long as we didn't throw bread at the table or start a fistfight outside the parlor windows, Mother gave us a good deal of leeway.

Grammaw knew that our manners were nothing to brag on. She said so, often and emphatically. But she

wanted the world to think that her grandsons were little
gentlemen who spoke only when spoken to and then remembered to add "sir" and "ma'am" without the gouge
of an elbow in their ribs. She would have liked to make
people think that Bru-Hubert and Hu-Bruce were boys
who sat around quietly and played guessing games in
order not to muss their clothes, and that at the table they
took the wing of the chicken by choice, rather than by
previous coaching.

It was usually at the dinner table that we capped the
climax, as Grammaw described it. We were right there
under people's noses, where everything we said or did
was sure to be noticed. Grammaw felt that if she got
through the meal without one of us disgracing her she
was safely over the hump of the day. Compared to Hubert and me, the other worries were only a drop in the
bucket.

Chod ate with the family, of course. His shaggy hair
and red, embarrassed face weren't exactly ornamental,
but at least he didn't say the wrong thing. He was a
man of few words. They were mostly "Yep," "Nope,"
and "Bruce and Hubert done it." He didn't have the
nerve to tattle on us in front of visitors, and so he ate
in silence and left the table as soon as he could.

Little Wilson was too young and appealing to be a
problem yet, and Devore was well-mannered. In fact, Devore often made the mistake of being overly polite. At
a company dinner there was always enough food for a
threshing crew, because farm women liked to hear guests

exclaim at the abundance and then pass it off with a care-
less remark, as though they had merely set out a light
snack. Sometimes a guest would praise the food and then
ask what we would do with everything that was left over.
Devore liked to put people at ease. Unless Grammaw's
swift foot found her shin in time, Devore was likely to
say cordially, "Oh, don't worry about leaving too much.
We'll live high for a week."

Hubert and I sat beyond Grammaw's kicking range.
She would caution us desperately beforehand and then
watch with gimlet eyes while she passed food and made
conversation, in order to head off our blunders. In spite
of her vigilance, however, we forgot and brought up sub-
jects that Grammaw thought were hidden for the day,
or I upset a dish, or Hubert accidentally belched, and
Grammaw wished she could go through the floor.

Grammaw had a special term for these breaches in our
manners, which she used after the guests had gone home
and she was raking us over the coals for the way we had
acted. "It 'pears to me you save up your very worst," she
reproached us angrily, "so you can *show your rumpuses*
when company comes." Usually she added, "I wish to
goodness I'd gone to live with your Aunt Clara instead
of comin' here. Be no heathenish boys there to plague
a-body's daylights out." Then she would sigh and tell
Mother she wondered why they even tried to live like
civilized folks. She said they ought to lock up the parlor
and tell people who wanted to visit us that we would not
be at home.

These pains vanished when the telephone rang to announce the next batch of visitors and she had the prospect of putting on style again. Grammaw was the happiest person on the place when she heard on a July morning, some months after my spectacular debut at Chapel Knob, that Mr. and Mrs. Snow of Chicago were going to favor us with their company at Sunday dinner.

Mr. Snow was head of the commission firm that handled Dad's strawberries. Often he came to Borden for several days during the picking season and went around the country to meet the growers. He had stopped at our place a number of times, but it was on business and he had never been closer to the house than the berry shed.

Mr. Snow took a liking to southern Indiana. He told Mother one day that he wanted to bring his wife down from Chicago later in the summer and show her this beautiful Knob Country. On the spur of the moment, Mother invited them to our house, and he accepted.

Mother had forgotten all about it until the Wednesday in July when she got a phone call from Borden. It was Mr. Snow reminding her of the invitation. He and Mrs. Snow were stopping at the McKinley Hotel a few days. They had bought a new Chalmers touring car and driven the long distance from Chicago. Mother said, "We'll expect you this coming Sunday for dinner." Then, in panic, she broke the news to Grammaw. Mother didn't feel capable of preparing a meal that would be up to their standards, or of entertaining them in our simple farm home.

Grammaw beamed. Rich people, *somebody*, from Chicago. An automobile in the front yard for the neighbors to see. The sky would be the limit to the food she could serve and to the style she could put on. Grammaw took a-holt.

The parlor was not only turned wrongside out and cleaned, but the lace curtains had to be done up fresh and the peafowl feathers removed from the vases and shaken and aired individually. Grammaw took the long round brush used for cleaning the cream-separator spouts and washed the seashells on the whatnot as far inside as she could gouge. She called Dad and Chod in and had them scoot the Beckwith forward a few inches in the alcove in order to display its grandeur more prominently. She was in favor of ripping up the carpet and changing the straw padding on the parlor floor. Mother told her there was no sense in going that far. She said they would have to take a chance on Mrs. Snow pulling out the tacks and looking under the carpet for dust.

Hubert and I were put to raking the grass and picking up fallen twigs from the sycamore tree. The brick walks had to be trimmed, and the weeds along the driveway pulled.

Mother and Grammaw planned the dinner and spent Saturday baking and cooking potatoes for salad and choosing the right pickles and preserves. Things were pretty well along by Saturday night, after we boys caught and picked the chickens and they were dressed and lowered in the well to keep cool.

Grammaw scrubbed the toilet with lye water. She said the Snows had traveled around the world, and there was no telling what fine toilets they had been in. On Sunday morning she tacked up a dozen more attractive scenic calendars and tore the scratchy colored pages out of the Sears' catalog.

She had looked up Chicago in our geography book as soon as she learned the Snows were coming and found some things to talk about. She didn't find a great deal of information. But Grammaw prepared to spread it thin.

By mid-morning, we kids were all scrubbed as clean as scraped potatoes. Grammaw took Hubert and me aside for our final instructions: "I'm goin' to use that nice tablecloth the pack peddlar gave your mother. Now, Bru-Hubert, when dinner's ready I don't want you to come swingin' around the door and holler, *'The white tablecloth we got from Joe!'* the way you did when Hamiltons' folks were here. Hu-Bruce, don't you let out a whoop, *'And buh-lackberry pie,'* like you do sometimes. Just walk in nice and set down and act like we have a linen tablecloth and pie every day. You don't need to talk. You can be seen and not heard. Don't tuck bread crusts under your plate and don't make slobbery noises over your water glasses. The crackers in that flowered dish are only for show; you can eat 'em afterward. And don't gulp your victuals like starved bloodhounds. There'll be plenty. Try your best not to show your rumpuses in front of Mr. and Mrs. Snow."

By ten o'clock, everything was ready. The cake and

pies were lined up on the pantry shelf. The dining table looked beautiful with the tablecloth we got from Joe, the best dishes, and the cut-glass preserve stands and spoon holders. The pots and kettles simmering on the kitchen stove held some of everything a 240-acre farm could produce. Mother slipped into a fresh dress and did her hair in a Psyche knot and added a pretty comb. Grammaw put on an embroidered black silk shirtwaist, her second-best black crepe skirt, with a frilly white organdy apron over it, and her Number One, or best, pair of shoes. She had donned her company face at daylight, but she began to draw it tighter and tighter as the morning wore on.

Hubert and I took turns sniffing the kitchen and climbing to our lookout to watch for the automobile. At eleven o'clock there was still no sign of it.

Mother wondered if there had been a misunderstanding about the date. She couldn't telephone and ask, because Miss Delia, the operator, would be at Sunday school and there was nobody at the switchboard to answer. Mother said, "Well, you know how city folks are. They don't go early in the morning for dinner like we do."

Grammaw said, "No, but I've just about give 'em out, haven't you?"

Grammaw went to make one last nervous inspection of the parlor. She was patting a sofa pillow when she heard a faint squeak from the direction of the organ. It startled Grammaw; she thought there must be a mouse in the instrument. If so, it was probably fixing to hide in the bellows till afternoon and then scamper out in the parlor while the company was being entertained. Be about her luck, Grammaw thought.

She hurried outdoors and snatched up the first cat she saw. She carried it to the parlor and pushed it around behind the organ. Grammaw was in a terrible hurry, and she expected the mouse to oblige her by running forth at once so the cat could catch it. The cat sniffed the carpet and meowed and rubbed against the back of the organ. It didn't seem to be interested in what was inside. Grammaw concluded that she had imagined the squeak.

"Come on out if you can't find a mouse," she told the cat, "and I'll carry you outdoors."

The cat meowed and sniffed, but it refused to come from behind the organ. Grammaw couldn't move the heavy instrument. She got down on her knees and felt around each side, but the cat kept out of reach of her groping hand. She called four-year-old Wilson, for he was tiny, and she was helping him scrounge behind the organ when—

"HERE THEY COME!" Hubert announced from the top of the sycamore tree.

A long streak of dust bubbled up from the road beyond Barksdales'. A haughty red Chalmers touring car sped down the hill and turned in at the gate. It crunched up at the driveway and came to a stop under the sycamore tree. Two stout, goggled figures wearing dusters climbed out.

Mr. Snow had a large robust chest and a large round stomach, and he walked so upright in carrying them both high in front that he had the appearance of leaning backward. Mrs. Snow had a large robust chest and a firm flat stomach. Under her duster she wore a dress of white eyelet embroidery. Her skin was beautiful; her dark eyes were friendly; she looked exactly the way we kids had always imagined a nice elderly queen would look. Mr. Snow was introducing her when Grammaw came to the front porch.

Grammaw said, "Pleased to make your acquaintance," in a high-pitched, cultured voice that didn't sound like it came from Grammaw. She shook hands on a level with her hairline and excused herself to go and make the sauce for the pudding while Mother and Dad ushered the Snows into the parlor to wait till dinner was ready.

It was a feast of the first magnitude. The chicken was so tender you could shake it off the bone. The dumplings were flaky. All the vegetables were fresh from the garden and at their best. There were dishes of deviled eggs and sliced tomatoes and slaw and lettuce and cottage cheese. There was pie or cake or pudding or all three to top it off.

Mr. and Mrs. Snow had big appetites. They piled up their plates and ate heartily. The food was good, but in spite of that the dinner didn't go right. The atmosphere seemed dead, and although Mr. and Mrs. Snow were polite it was plain that they weren't having a good time. There was a feeling around the table that the Snows considered themselves too good for the company of farmers. Mrs. Snow did compliment Mother and Grammaw on their cooking. "And there's so *much* of everything," she exclaimed.

Devore winced and looked under the table at her leg, while Grammaw passed a dish and said, "Have some of this crabapple jelly."

Mother and Dad tried to bring things to life, and Grammaw worked so hard putting on style that soon a bright pink spot glowed on each side of her screwed-up face. She used the biggest words she knew, and she was careful to say "I presumed" when she meant "I 'loud," and "almost entirely" instead of her usual "put-near." Every once in a while she threw in a fact about Chicago. Her little finger on her coffee cup pointed straight to the hook in the ceiling that held the hanging lamp. She watched Hubert and me.

Once or twice I started to say something, but I got a quick glassy stare from Grammaw, and her frown looked for a moment as though she had chewed up a lump of salt in her biscuit. Hubert belched once, but it was only a tiny surface belch, instead of one of his rumbles that seemed to come from the bowels of the earth, and Grammaw was able to cover it by quickly clearing her throat and uttering a polite cough.

Chod's fork went up and down in the same steady rhythm he used both for eating and scooping grain into a bag. As soon as he had shoveled himself full enough to tie, he pushed back his chair and left.

Finally, Mr. and Mrs. Snow protested that they couldn't eat another bite of steamed pudding or pie or drink another cup of coffee. They laid down their napkins, and Mother rose and led the way to the parlor.

Dad and Mr. Snow lit cigars. Everybody just sat. There wasn't much to say. Of course, if the farm was mentioned, Grammaw steered the talk away from that subject. It was too lowly for the Snows. Mrs. Snow asked about our cows, saying it must be wonderful to churn such fine butter from your own herd. Grammaw remembered from the geography book the average yearly number of cattle shipped to Chicago. She gave the figure.

After a while Mrs. Snow asked about the wild flowers growing in the Knob woods. She had heard of the great variety of them. Someone in Borden had mailed her a box of those gorgeous big purple violets. Grammaw liked the violets, too, but they were local and therefore far too common to talk about. She barely acknowledged the presence of violets in our woods and then reached to the bottom of the barrel for an item on Chicago. The only subject she could scrape up was railroads. It didn't exactly fit the purple violets, but she told how many main lines entered the city, and named a few. Mrs. Snow was quite polite, but her expression hinted that she didn't care how many railroads entered Chicago or, for that matter, how many left it.

Grammaw said, "Boys," to Hubert and me. She raised her eyebrows and in a way that only she could do she pointed with them to the door. Grammaw wanted us to go out and play. The air in the parlor was tense, and she thought it was about time for one of us to make a bad break. Hubert and I didn't want to go out and play. We wanted to stand where we could see Mr. Snow's gold watch chain and Mrs. Snow's diamond rings. Grammaw asked them if they would like to look through the stereoscope. They said they believed not, just now.

Little Wilson was playing around on the floor, down on all fours in imitation of a pony. By and by he crawled into the alcove behind the organ. He stuck his head out and yelled, "Grammaw!" His eyes were popping. *"Grammaw!"*

"What is it, Wilson?" Grammaw asked above the dead silence of the room.

"You remember that cat you brought back here this morning?"

It took Grammaw by surprise, for in the ordeal of putting on style it had slipped her mind.

"A cat?" she asked, giving a nervous little laugh of remembrance. She blushed the color of a pickled beet, already mortified at the thought of what Wilson was about to announce, although she could have sworn that all of our cats were housebroken. "Why, yes. Oh, yes, a cat. Ha-ha. I have a slight recollection of the incident, but I presumed it had immediately—uh—Wilson, you come right out from behind that organ-Mrs.-Snow-you-must-see-these-views-of-Yellowstone-Park." She grabbed the stereoscope and poked it into Mrs. Snow's face.

Wilson wasn't to be shut up so easily. He was bursting with news: "Well, there's six of 'em back here now: that same big cat and five little bitty ones chewing the buttons off her vest."

The shock was so different from the one Grammaw had braced herself against that for the first time that day she lost control.

"Merciful Father!" she exclaimed, giving her leg a hard slap with the palm of her hand. "I plumb forgot that pot-bellied hussy."

Mr. and Mrs. Snow gazed at the ceiling. They bit their lips. Their faces crinkled around the eyes and they burst into laughter. They bent over double and shrieked. It was such a genuine, really tickled kind of laughter that everybody, including Grammaw, joined in. As an ice-breaker, Grammaw's slip of the tongue had been more effective than a stick of dynamite.

Mr. and Mrs. Snow liked cats. They insisted on taking a look at the baby kittens, so Dad and Mr. Snow pulled the organ out of its alcove into the middle of the parlor. Grammaw relaxed and put on her comfortable everyday face, and she was soon taking the Snows out in the back-yard to meet a couple of dozen more of our cats. They asked to go and see the cows and horses.

Mrs. Snow squeezed into one of Mother's calico dresses and covered the wide gap in front with Grammaw's loud-est green paisley apron. Mr. Snow squeezed as far as he could into a pair of Dad's overalls. They went tramping with us to the barn and to the pasture. They picked daisies in the cherry orchard; they drank water at the spring. The afternoon passed quicker than a picnic.

They agreed to stay for supper if we would eat leftovers and Mrs. Snow could help with the dishes. It was long after dark when they left, with a promise, which they kept, of coming back next summer.

The funny thing was, after they had buttoned on their dusters and were about to climb into the automobile, Mrs. Snow impulsively threw her arms around Grammaw's neck and kissed her good-bye.

The lights swung out into the road, and the Chalmers roared away.

Grammaw said, "Weren't they sweet? Sure not stuck-up like I 'loud people from Chicago would be."

9

Grammaw Changes Beds

EVERY SO OFTEN GRAMMAW SPOKE OF LEAVING OUR HOUSE
and going to live with Aunt Clara. I don't mean to say
she discussed it with Mother and Dad. The only time she
spoke of it was when Hubert and I did something to ag-
gravate her. Then she told us firmly that if we didn't
take to doing better she would move to Aunt Clara's.

She always mentioned this particular daughter because
her home offered the greatest contrast to farm life that
Grammaw could think of. Aunt Clara and Uncle Walton,
who owned a real estate business, lived in what we knew
from descriptions to be a huge red brick house with a
mansard roof and fancy iron trimmings. In the minds of
us kids, "Aunt Clara's house" stood for a kind of rich
grandeur such as we pictured when mention was made
of the Queen's palace in a book. However, it wasn't the
Oriental rugs and mahogany furniture that tempted
Grammaw to leave the farm and go to Evansville. Aunt
Clara and Uncle Walton had no children, and Grammaw
assured Hubert and me that the absence of boys like us
was what made their home so attractive to her.

Hardly a day went by that she didn't remind us of it.
Whenever we sassed her, or ran through her flowerbeds,

or neglected our work, or bloodied each other's nose in a fistfight, or accidentally dumped little Wilson out of the wheelbarrow, or did any of the other things that we took pleasure in doing, Grammaw flew off her handle and threatened to leave. In the same tone of voice she'd once used when promising to take a peach-tree switch and cut us to the red she announced, "I won't stay here another week. If you have to behave like a couple of heathens I'll pack up and go to your Aunt Clara's, where a-body can live in peace."

There was hardly a night when she didn't use the same threat to quiet us down after we went upstairs to bed. Hubert and I would start to rassle when we undressed. If one of us thumped the floor too hard and jarred the windows a bit, Grammaw's door banged open, and we heard the quick patter of her carpet slippers across the hall. We jumped in bed, and of course we squinted through our eyelashes and pretended to be asleep when Grammaw's ruffled nightcap and enraged face appeared in our door.

"Now, you boys better quiet down in here," she spluttered. "You won't be half so brisk when it comes time to get up in the morning." Getting no answer except mock snores of the long-drawn-out, whistling type, she added, "And I beg to inform you that I'm leavin' here. I'll go to your Aunt Clara's, where I won't have to listen to a hurrah and a hubbub till way in the night." She slammed the door.

Grammaw knew that she would be welcome at Aunt Clara's because Aunt Clara did everything she could to lure her away from our house. She and Uncle Walton came for a visit each year, arriving splendidly on the train with a number of polished leather suitcases full of fine clothes we kids were not permitted to touch. Aunt Clara was dainty and pretty and always dressed in the latest fashion. One summer she shocked Grammaw by wearing a hobble skirt with a long slit that revealed a triangle of her taffeta petticoat when she walked. Uncle Walton was tall and slim and had his hair parted in the middle; his skin was the transparent, milk-white color of a potato sprout grown in a dark cellar.

They couldn't understand why Mamma, as they called her, wanted to live in the country. Oh, the country was all right; in fact, it was a wonderful place for farmers, if they hadn't had to work so hard; but there were too many things like mad bulls and gypsies and snakes and runaway horses for a woman of Mamma's age to contend with. Not to mention the annoyances that seemed to come in *pairs*. Aunt Clara shuddered; she thought Hubert and I were dumb as well as obnoxious. And a farmhouse heated with fireplaces was drafty in the wintertime; there was no telling when Mamma would take pneumonia. Aunt Clara and Uncle Walton had a lovely bedroom on the first floor of their house, so Mamma wouldn't have to climb stairs. And a bathroom, so Mamma wouldn't have to trot to the garden in all kinds of weather. And a hired girl, so Mamma wouldn't have to do housework. "Mamma, you're not getting any younger, you know," Aunt Clara reminded her.

Grammaw always made the same excuse for not going

home with them. She dreaded to undertake the tiresome all-day journey to Evansville. To get there from our house, you had to go to Borden and catch the morning train to Town—a one-coach train known as the Accommodation because it obligingly stopped at every tiny depot along the Monon line. After a long wait in Town you changed cars and traveled over a bumpy little spur of the Southern to a junction near Evansville and rode the rest of the way in a public hack. Grammaw had never ridden on a train, and she told Aunt Clara she was jooberous about trying it.

She didn't tell Hubert and me how she expected to travel when she left the farm and went to make her home at Aunt Clara's. But go she would, she declared whenever she got her dander up, just as sure as we didn't mend our ways.

After the Snows' visit (highly successful from Grammaw's point of view because, for once, we had failed to disgrace her) her attitude seemed to relax. And then on a rainy September morning when Hubert and I were forced to stay indoors, the storm broke.

Hubert and I had recently chosen new careers. Shortly after my performance at Chapel Knob we had abandoned the idea of becoming cowboys, either musical or non-musical, and elected to be surgeons, instead. We were tired of experimenting on dead and dried-up field-mice, and it occurred to us that one of Devore's dolls would make an excellent specimen.

Devore had outgrown dolls, but in her meticulous way she had saved every one of them, from the first Raggedy

Ann of battered calico to the final and elegant Rebecca, who would gently lower her porcelain eyelids and squeak, "Ma-ma." Devore was still planning to be a nurse, and we naturally assumed that she would be willing to make a small sacrifice for the cause of Medicine. So we saw no reason to ask her permission before we went to her closet shelf and got Rebecca. We had just begun an exploratory operation when all of a sudden Rebecca hemorrhaged a great pile of sawdust on Grammaw's freshly polished dining-room floor. For this double offense, Grammaw jumped on us with more vigor than usual, and we answered her in like manner.

"Don't you sass me!" she shouted. "I'll give you to understand I don't have to stay here and take your slack. You just dare talk to me like that again and I'll go to your Aunt Clara's, where I can be treated with some respect."

"Nobody's stopping you," Hubert blurted out.

"The road's open," I told her. "Go right ahead."

"That's enough!" Grammaw exploded. "I'll leave this place, I will, just as sure as God made little apples."

Usually, such a heated exchange of words merely meant that Grammaw and Hubert and I were all three feeling up to par. She corrected us in her violent way; we flared up and sassed her; she threatened to start packing her clothes; and a few minutes later the harsh words were forgiven.

Grammaw didn't forgive us that day. She went upstairs right after supper, saying she had a letter to write. She didn't tell us who it was to, but before the end of the week the mailman brought her a big cream-colored envelope with Aunt Clara's monogram.

Grammaw read the letter twice, and then she said to Mother, "Clara and Walton are coming up Saturday. They'll be here till Monday and—well, Lulie, I reckon I'll go home with 'em."

"It ought to be a nice visit. How long do you expect to stay?"

Grammaw answered firmly, "I'm goin' for good."

"Oh no, Ma," Mother exclaimed. "You don't mean you're leaving us?"

"Anyhow for the winter, and then I'll see how I feel about it in the spring. The canning is finished and most of the other fall work's done up. Devore's sixteen and big enough to manage the cookin'. I don't think I'm needed here."

"It isn't a question of being needed. We want you. I thought you considered this your home."

"I figure it's time I made a change, that's all," Grammaw said, taking care not to look at Hubert and me. "Clara has been devilin' me for a good many years to come and live with her. So now I'm goin'."

"It's for you to decide," Mother said; and then as if to dissuade her she added, "But, Ma, you always claimed you were afraid of riding on the train."

"I won't have to worry about the train," Grammaw answered. "It so happens that Walton has bought an automobile. Clara says they plan to drive."

Aunt Clara and Uncle Walton arrived with a flourish on Saturday afternoon in a high-waisted Buick roadster

with red wheels and a great deal of brass and leather trim.
Aunt Clara was so happy that Grammaw had at last come
to her senses after four and a half years and decided to
leave the farm.

"Notice how frail poor Mamma looks," she said to
Uncle Walton. "I'm going to see that she takes a good
long rest the first thing."

Grammaw bustled around most of the day Sunday,
sorting clothes and packing; she hardly took time to speak
to Hubert and me. She was still quiet on Monday morning when she came downstairs dressed to leave, and
Uncle Walton began to stow her luggage in the automobile. The assortment was enough to raise Aunt Clara's
eyebrows. There were two split-baskets and the old canvas valise, half a dozen pasteboard cartons, an overflowing work basket, and all kinds of lumpy, odd-sized parcels
containing her trinkets and keepsakes and the quilt pieces
that would keep her winter days occupied. And, although
it was early in the season, she had dug a number of her
favorite red dahlias and wrapped the bulbs in newspaper.
Grammaw was evidently preparing to stay longer than
one winter.

When it came time to go, she kissed Devore and little
Wilson and Mother; she shook hands with Dad and told
Chod good-bye. Then she pecked Hubert and me on the
cheek and climbed up in the seat between Aunt Clara
and Uncle Walton. We all stood in the yard and watched
the automobile speed up the hill and pass the persimmon
tree, taking Grammaw away from us. The leather top
dipped below the brow of the hill; Grammaw's fluttering

black veil disappeared; and she was gone. Mother dabbed at her eyes and turned and went into the house.

Hubert and I spent the day in the woods picking up hickory nuts, and so we hardly thought of Grammaw until we went upstairs at bedtime. We started a pillow fight, and as there was no one to stop us we rassled around until we had feathers strewn all over the floor. We laughed and laughed. Hubert said, "Boy, it sure is wonderful not to have somebody come across the hall and scream at us every time we make a little noise."

I said, "Boy, it sure is," and we laughed some more as we blew out the light and went to bed.

The night was dark and quiet. A cool breeze, full of the harvest odors of September, puffed in through the west windows. It felt good to snuggle in the feather bed and enjoy the cozy warmth of an extra quilt.

Outside in the sycamore tree a solitary katydid began its low, rasping call, "Katy-did-Katy-didn't-Katy-did-Katy-didn't." You could fall into the rhythm anywhere and no matter which one you started on, the quick, endless phrases would alternate "did" and "didn't" as long as you lay awake and listened. "Katy-did-Katy-didn't-Katy-did-Katy-didn't." What was it that Grammaw always told us when we heard the first one on a midsummer night? Oh yes, she said it would be six weeks till frost. "Katy-did-Katy-didn't." It had a note of sadness and premonition I had never noticed before. I wondered if there were katydids in Evansville. I wondered if Grammaw would be listening to them as she lay in her rich bedroom at Aunt Clara's house. I wondered if she would ever think of us boys at bedtime. Probably not; she always got mad at us, and so she would naturally want to forget us. Across the hall, the door to Grammaw's room stood open. I heard her Seth Thomas clock, busy and brisk, ticking off the minutes the way it had ticked off all the nights Grammaw had spent there. But the room wasn't the same. For the first time, I couldn't hear the small, familiar sounds of Grammaw moving around as she prepared to go to bed. Without them, the room seemed awful empty.

"Katy-did-Katy-didn't," the lonesome call went on and on in the cool whispering darkness.

I lay and listened to the clock and the katydid and the black night. I thought Hubert had gone to sleep. After a while he said, "How far is it to Evansville?"

"I don't know," I said. "It must be a heck of a long ways. Why?"

"Oh, I just wondered. Say, that clock ticks loud, doesn't it?"

"Yeah, it sure does. A clock always sounds loud in an empty room."

The next day brought our first real Indian Summer weather. The sun was warm in a cool sea-blue sky. The hills and hollows glowed with color, and a soft gray haze curtained the horizon. It was one of those quiet, brooding fall days when a sense of peaceful completeness enfolds the world.

But for some reason, Hubert and I felt out of sorts. Instead of going to the woods to pick up hickory nuts, we stayed close to the house.

It was odd not to see Grammaw whisking about the
yard, hanging dishtowels on the fence, snipping flowers
for a bouquet, whip-cracking the dust out of a rug. It was
odd not to hear Grammaw yelling at us to bring cookstove wood, singing out "Hi-yah, Dewey" from the back
steps to call the dog to his breakfast, making a big racket
in the separator house over the scouring of the milk
buckets.

Hubert and I got our ball and bat and started a game
of tippy-up near the kitchen. Now was the time when
Grammaw ought to come flying out the door like a mad
hen and holler, "Take that infernal ball away from the
house before you break another window light." Grammaw wasn't there; she wouldn't come flying out.

We put away the ball and bat and went upstairs to
rummage in her room. We were too old for such a pas-
time, but this exploration of her treasures had never lost
its interest. The place was neat and clean, but it looked
bare. The walls had been stripped of all the gay colored
objects that made the room seem like Grammaw. We
went through her dresser drawers, turning over the few
ribbons and quilt scraps and half-empty spools of thread
she had left, but our hearts weren't in it. We didn't have
to tiptoe around and avoid the squeaky board in the floor
that would give us away and bring Grammaw at a gallop
to chase us out. It wasn't Grammaw's room anymore. No,
Grammaw had moved to Evansville, and she wouldn't be
coming back.

At the dinner table I noticed what a big gap one tiny
person can leave in a family circle. Devore had forgotten

and put a plate for her when she set the table, but there was nobody at the corner, the place where Grammaw had always sat, with the coffee pot at her elbow on an upside-down pie tin. It was no use to keep glancing up at the kitchen door in hopes that Grammaw would appear. Grammaw was eating at Aunt Clara's, where the coffee was poured by the hired girl, and she could put on style every day of the week.

Grammaw's flowers had always made our yard so cheer-ful, but now without her they looked sad. The cannas were dabs of red and gold, as bright as ever against the white fence. The pink and white and lavender faces of the cosmos gazed over the pickets, just as they had yester-day. The spikes of flowering sage were the same little rows of flames above the dark foliage. But there in the zinnia beds, heavy-headed and brown above the streamers of torn rag tied to their stems, hung the drying blooms that Grammaw had marked to save for seed. She had for-gotten to pick them.

Late in the afternoon, Hubert and I climbed up to our lookout to wait for the Accommodation. It came out from Town and went through Borden at four o'clock. We couldn't see the train itself on account of the Knobs, but we could hear the engine and trace its route up the valley by the smoke it made.

Beneath us the fire-bright colors of sumac and sassa-fras and Virginia creeper lined the roads and spotted the fields as far as we could see. The surface of the Knob woods rolled away to the north like a vast hit-and-miss rag carpet—hickory-brown, maple-scarlet, and poplar-yellow, woven with the dark green chain of pine and cedar. An odor of leaf smoke from out of nowhere sifted through the branches of the sycamore. Somewhere a long ways off, the hum of a silo filler rose and fell on the drowsy air.

Now we could stay up in our lookout as long as we wanted to. Grammaw wouldn't yell at us to bring her a few cobs or a handful of kindling or invent some flimsy errand to get us down out of the tree for fear a limb would break and we would fall and bust ourselves.

It was a perfect time to sit and dream and make believe. We had outgrown Sir Galahad and Jim Hawkins, but the lookout was still our favorite retreat. We sat for a long time without saying a word. We had the blues, and there wasn't any doubt now about the reason. We missed Grammaw till we could hardly stand it.

I thought of the years she had lived at our house, and I felt terrible about all the trouble Hubert and I had caused her. . . .

. . . Way back in the beginning, Grammaw had expected us to be little granddaughters who would sit around and behave and learn to sew and crochet. So the first act of our lives was to disappoint her, and as we grew older and rougher and more resourceful in ways to plague her we had never done a thing to make her change her mind and really love us. . . .

. . . Finally, we became so mean and sassy she couldn't put up with us any longer. She'd warned us a thousand times that she would leave, but Grammaw was hot-tempered the same as we were, and we never believed she meant it. Besides, we knew that she was too scared of trains to travel far. . . .

. . . Grammaw got as mad as a hornet when we misbehaved, but she had never once in our lives tattled on us. Even when she packed up and left she didn't say a word against us. She just told Mother she thought it was time she made a change. . . .

. . . I would have given anything in the world if I could have taken back the cruel words that had driven her away. How good and quiet and obedient I would be if only Grammaw would come back. I wouldn't complain about having to work. I would even try to make her feel glad that I hadn't been a girl. . . .

. . . I wondered if I could write her a letter in care of Aunt Clara and say I was sorry. It probably wouldn't do any good. Maybe sometime I would be lucky enough to break a leg, or a horse would run over me, as Grammaw had always predicted, and Mother would send for her. . . .

. . . Aunt Clara had taken her to Evansville, away from her grandsons and all the aggravations of the farm. After she once got used to a life of luxury and quiet in Aunt Clara's house she wouldn't want to be bothered about us. Perhaps she wouldn't even come back if one of us died.

These things went around and around in my mind as we sat in silence and dangled our legs and looked at the melancholy fall scenery. I didn't say anything to Hubert. I wondered what he was thinking. All at once he blew his nose with a loud conk and said bitterly, "I wish I'd never heard of old Aunt Clara."

A moment later the Accommodation whistled, and we saw a long curving banner of smoke and steam ripple up from the valley. The train coasted into Borden and screeched to a stop. We could hear the engine panting, as though it might be getting its wind while the passengers climbed off and the express was unloaded. Then a puff of smoke, followed by a slam of steam, and the Accommodation pulled out of Borden and chugged up the valley.

This was the time of day when Grammaw always made her first call for us to come and start carrying the night's supply of spring water. Usually we sassed her and stayed up in the lookout until we could no longer hear the train. We liked to pretend that we were on the Accommodation, leaning back against the bottle-green plush cushions and riding through cinders and dipping telephone wires all the way to Bloomington. But today, in obedience to some impulse we couldn't explain, we climbed down and went to the kitchen for our water buckets. We were just in time to hear the telephone ring a long-and-two-shorts. Mother had come into the house to build a fire and help Devore start supper. She answered it.

"Hello. . . . Yes, it is. . . . What? . . . For goodness' sakes, what's wrong?"

A sudden fear hit me like a fist in my stomach. Something had happened to Grammaw. Maybe an automobile accident.

"Listen," Hubert said.

Mother went on, "Where are you? . . . Why are you down there? . . . You aren't sick, are you? . . . I thought you were in Evansville. . . . What? . . . Why, yes, of course he will. I'll have the boys go and tell him. He ought to be there in an hour."

Mother hung up and told us that Grammaw was in Borden. Mother didn't know why, or how she had arrived there. She only knew that Grammaw was at the McKinley Hotel, waiting for Dad to come and get her.

"Maybe she forgot something," Mother suggested, puzzled. "You know as much about it as I do. Go and tell Dad."

Hubert sped to the cornfield to break the news while I hitched Old Nellie to the buggy. Dad drove away in a hurry without stopping to change his overalls.

Hubert and I wrenched the milk out of the cows and whizzed it through the separator and then we climbed up to our lookout again. We waited and watched the road at the church. The sun went past the belfry and slid down behind the tallest of the gravestones. We waited and watched. The sun was slicing into the pale, smoky horizon when Old Nellie finally appeared among the willow trees. The buggy disappeared in the hollow at Barksdales' and cleared the hill above the persimmon tree. There was the small familiar figure beside Dad on the buggy seat.

"She's with him!" Hubert cried. "It's Grammaw!"

We ran to meet them as they came up the driveway. I thought of that spring day when Grammaw first came to live at our house, and I remembered how eagerly Hubert and I had gone to welcome her. But not half as eagerly as we were going now.

Grammaw wasn't quite so erect anymore in her severe black, and her face under the perennial little round hat and veil seemed tired and more deeply lined, but her blue eyes had lost none of their pertness. She was looking the place over carefully as they came up the driveway, not with the darting, inquisitive glance of a newly arrived bird this time, but with the peaceful, lingering examination of a person who is returning home. I knew even before I saw her luggage that Grammaw hadn't come back for something she had forgotten. She had come back because of things she didn't want to forget.

The front screen slammed, and Mother ran down the walk, followed by Devore and little Wilson.

"Why, Ma," Mother said, for want of a better way to express her surprise at Grammaw's sudden return, "what are you doing here?"

"Gettin' out of the buggy," Grammaw answered, suiting the action to the words. "What does it look like I'm doin'?"

"We missed you," Mother said. "But what was wrong with Evansville?"

Grammaw said in a matter-of-fact voice, "Not a thing was wrong with Evansville that I know of."

"Didn't you like Clara's house?"

"It's the finest house I was ever in. Carpets you sink in clear up to your ankles; furniture shines till you can see to part your hair in it."

"Weren't Clara and Walton good to you?"

"Certainly they were good to me. They waited on me hand and foot."

"How did you get to Borden?" Mother asked next.

"I got there on the Accommodation."

"You mean you came out from Town on it?"

"I did."

"How did you get to Town?"

"Trains go both ways, don't they?"

"You rode there on the Southern?"

Grammaw's voice was gruff. "I did."

"Weren't you scared, all by yourself?"

Grammaw's voice was gruffer still. "I was."

"Have you come back to stay?" Mother asked, as Dad unloaded pasteboard cartons.

"I have."

"I'm glad, Ma. But I can't understand why you would come on the train when the folks have that lovely new automobile. That's a tiresome trip, changing trains in Town and everything."

"I came on the train because I wanted to come today. Walton couldn't leave his office till next Saturday."

"They were expecting you to spend the winter. What did they think when you turned around and came right back after staying only one night?"

"I didn't ask 'em what they thought. I told 'em I was comin' home. Anyhow, there wasn't much they could do about it. My mind was made up. I reckon I'm old enough to be my own boss, ain't I?"

Grammaw turned away from Mother and picked up her valise.

"Bru-Hubert," she said. "Help me take my things in-side. Hu-Bruce, are you goin' to stand there all night gawkin'? Bring some of them boxes."

We carried her luggage upstairs, the same assortment, down to the last parcel, that she had taken away. Gram-maw followed us, and all at once the deserted four walls became Grammaw's room again.

She changed to an everyday black calico dress and a brilliant red and green checkered apron and bustled downstairs. She had brought a gift for each of us kids: a hair ribbon for Devore, a monkey on a string for little Wilson, and a Barlow knife apiece for Hubert and me.

"Now see which one of you can cut a finger off first," she said, and hurried to the kitchen.

"Devore, did you salt these potatoes?" I heard the sizzle of a skillet, the rattle of a granite lid as Grammaw added more coffee to the pot. My throat was lumpy, but my heart was light.

Mother could see that Grammaw wasn't ready to talk about it, and so she didn't press her for an explanation of the sudden change in her plans. We learned piecemeal about her journey from Evansville.

She had made Uncle Walton drive her to the junction that morning and put her on the train—the jolty little spur of the Southern. It was her first time on a railway car. Equally fearful of robbers and of train wrecks, she rode to Town with her hands on her pocketbook and her mind on the Good Lord. Grammaw had always been so confused by the noise and hurry of a city, with its autos and streetcars and shops. Yet she managed to find the

Monon depot clear on the other side of Town. Being timid about taking a streetcar, she carried her valise and walked, stopping now and then to ask for directions. She placed the valise on a bench in the waiting room and asked the ticket agent to keep an eye on it while she trudged back across Town to the Southern depot for the baskets. She left them on the bench and made two more trips for the pasteboard cartons and the odd parcels of keepsakes and quilt pieces and dahlia bulbs. Buying and eating a meal alone in a restaurant presented too much of a problem, so she sat in the station and nibbled cheese and crackers out of a paper bag until train time. Then at last she got aboard the Accommodation and rode triumphantly to Borden. And she had cheerfully gone through this ordeal because she wanted to come home *today*, rather than wait till the end of the week and be brought easily and swiftly to the door in Uncle Walton's Buick. And except for short visits she never again left the farm until that sad morning when we took her back to Horner's Chapel to remain with Grandpa.

One winter day after her journey to Evansville, Mother and Grammaw were sitting by the fireplace cutting carpet rags when I heard Mother say casually, "Ma, you never did tell us why you didn't stay but one night at Clara's."

"Well, Lulie," Grammaw said, hesitating, "that night after Clara and Walton had gone to sleep, and the house was so quiet, I was layin' there wide awake and I happened to remember, I always heard it wasn't good for a-body my age to change beds."

About the Author

W. BRUCE BELL LIVES ON A SMALL FARM IN HIS HOMETOWN OF Borden, Indiana, the setting for the adventures in this book. He received his bachelor's degree from DePauw University and has worked in a variety of jobs, ranging from office clerk to French teacher. But his greatest interest has proved to be music, which he has taught either full time or as a hobby for fifty years. "I cannot resist a talented piano pupil," he says, "and consequently I have never been able to retire." *A Little Dab of Color* is Mr. Bell's first children's book.